IF I WERE YOU

SELECTED FICTION WORKS BY L. RON HUBBARD

FANTASY

SCIENCE FICTION

ADVENTURE

WESTERN

A full list of L. Ron Hubbard's
novellas and short stories is provided at the back.

*Dekalogy—a group of ten volumes

L. RON HUBBARD

If I Were You

GALAXY PRESS

Published by
Galaxy Press, LLC
7051 Hollywood Boulevard, Suite 200
Hollywood, CA 90028

Printed in the United States of America.

ISBN-10 1-59212-359-7
ISBN-13 978-1-59212-359-9

Library of Congress Control Number: 2007927523

CONTENTS

STORIES FROM PULP FICTION'S GOLDEN AGE

A ND it *was* a golden age.

The 1930s and 1940s were a vibrant, seminal time for a gigantic audience of eager readers, probably the largest per capita audience of readers in American history. The magazine racks were chock-full of publications with ragged trims, garish cover art, cheap brown pulp paper, low cover prices—and the most excitement you could hold in your hands.

"Pulp" magazines, named for their rough-cut, pulpwood paper, were a vehicle for more amazing tales than Scheherazade could have told in a million and one nights. Set apart from higher-class "slick" magazines, printed on fancy glossy paper with quality artwork and superior production values, the pulps were for the "rest of us," adventure story after adventure story for people who liked to *read*. Pulp fiction authors were no-holds-barred entertainers—real storytellers. They were more interested in a thrilling plot twist, a horrific villain or a white-knuckle adventure than they were in lavish prose or convoluted metaphors.

The sheer volume of tales released during this wondrous golden age remains unmatched in any other period of literary history—hundreds of thousands of published stories in over nine hundred different magazines. Some titles lasted only an issue or two; many magazines succumbed to paper shortages during World War II, while others endured for decades yet. Pulp fiction remains as a treasure trove of stories you can read, stories you can love, stories you can remember. The stories were driven by plot and character, with grand heroes, terrible villains, beautiful damsels (often in distress), diabolical plots, amazing places, breathless romances. The readers wanted to be taken beyond the mundane, to live adventures far removed from their ordinary lives—and the pulps rarely failed to deliver.

In that regard, pulp fiction stands in the tradition of all memorable literature. For as history has shown, good stories are much more than fancy prose. William Shakespeare, Charles Dickens, Jules Verne, Alexandre Dumas—many of the greatest literary figures wrote their fiction for the readers, not simply literary colleagues and academic admirers. And writers for pulp magazines were no exception. These publications reached an audience that dwarfed the circulations of today's short story magazines. Issues of the pulps were scooped up and read by over thirty million avid readers each month.

Because pulp fiction writers were often paid no more than a cent a word, they had to become prolific or starve. They also had to write aggressively. As Richard Kyle, publisher and editor of *Argosy*, the first and most long-lived of the pulps, so pointedly explained: "The pulp magazine writers, the best of them, worked for markets that did not write for critics or attempt to satisfy timid advertisers. Not having to answer to anyone other than their readers, they wrote about human beings on the edges of the unknown, in those new lands the future would explore. They wrote for what we would become, not for what we had already been."

Some of the more lasting names that graced the pulps include H. P. Lovecraft, Edgar Rice Burroughs, Robert E. Howard, Max Brand, Louis L'Amour, Elmore Leonard, Dashiell Hammett, Raymond Chandler, Erle Stanley Gardner, John D. MacDonald, Ray Bradbury, Isaac Asimov, Robert Heinlein—and, of course, L. Ron Hubbard.

In a word, he was among the most prolific and popular writers of the era. He was also the most enduring—hence this series—and certainly among the most legendary. It all began only months after he first tried his hand at fiction, with L. Ron Hubbard tales appearing in *Thrilling Adventures, Argosy, Five-Novels Monthly, Detective Fiction Weekly, Top-Notch, Texas Ranger, War Birds, Western Stories,* even *Romantic Range.* He could write on any subject, in any genre, from jungle explorers to deep-sea divers, from G-men and gangsters, cowboys and flying aces to mountain climbers, hard-boiled detectives and spies. But he really began to shine when he turned his talent to science fiction and fantasy of which he authored nearly fifty novels or novelettes to forever change the shape of those genres.

Following in the tradition of such famed authors as Herman Melville, Mark Twain, Jack London and Ernest Hemingway, Ron Hubbard actually lived adventures that his own characters would have admired—as an ethnologist among primitive tribes, as prospector and engineer in hostile climes, as a captain of vessels on four oceans. He even wrote a series of articles for *Argosy,* called "Hell Job," in which he lived and told of the most dangerous professions a man could put his hand to.

Finally, and just for good measure, he was also an accomplished photographer, artist, filmmaker, musician and educator. But he was first and foremost a *writer,* and that's the L. Ron Hubbard we come to know through the pages of this volume.

This library of Stories from the Golden Age presents the best of L. Ron Hubbard's fiction from the heyday of storytelling, the Golden Age of the pulp magazines. In these eighty volumes, readers are treated to a full banquet of 153 stories, a kaleidoscope of tales representing every imaginable genre: science fiction, fantasy, western, mystery, thriller, horror, even romance—action of all kinds and in all places.

Because the pulps themselves were printed on such inexpensive paper with high acid content, issues were not meant to endure. As the years go by, the original issues of every pulp from *Argosy* through *Zeppelin Stories* continue crumbling into brittle, brown dust. This library preserves the L. Ron Hubbard tales from that era, presented with a distinctive look that brings back the nostalgic flavor of those times.

L. Ron Hubbard's Stories from the Golden Age has something for every taste, every reader. These tales will return you to a time when fiction was good clean entertainment and the most fun a kid could have on a rainy afternoon or the best thing an adult could enjoy after a long day at work.

Pick up a volume, and remember what reading is supposed to be all about. Remember curling up with a *great story.*

—Kevin J. Anderson

KEVIN J. ANDERSON *is the author of more than ninety critically acclaimed works of speculative fiction, including* The Saga of Seven Suns, *the continuation of the Dune Chronicles with Brian Herbert, and his* New York Times *bestselling novelization of L. Ron Hubbard's* Ai! Pedrito!

IF I WERE YOU

If I Were You

FITTINGLY, it was a dark and blustery night when the Professor died. The summer storm had come yelling in from a scorching afternoon to tear at canvas and yank out stakes and stab bright fury at the big top. The rain bucketed down with a shock of coldness and then settled to a ceaseless cannonading which, after seven hours, had turned the lot into a swamp so tenacious that not even the rubber mules could budge the wagons. Banners wept from their staffs; lot lice shivered in scant cover; somewhere a big cat, excited by the tropical aspect of the storm, moaned and paced in his cage.

And although a waxen yellowness was already upon his face and his skin was falling away from his bones, the Professor managed an evil smile. He was waiting, hanging on and waiting. For he had sent half an hour since for Little Tom Little, king of the midgets. And as he waited, his thoughts roamed over the past, the better to savor what he was about to do.

The Professor was the gypsy camp's bird of bad omen. Whence he had come, no man knew, but with him had come a chain of disaster. Tall and bony, he had always been more a cadaver than a man; his scummed eyes hid behind thick, dark lids; his hands seemed always ready to throttle a victim;

3

his black hair was matted about his face, just as his clothes were matted about his form.

He had come as a mitt reader. Mrs. Johnson had not wanted to take him but, boss of the show though she was, she had not been able to refuse him. Hermann Schmidt, ringmaster and governor de facto, powerful figure though he was, had been unable to resist the eerie command of those eyes. And the man had become "The Professor" to the gypsy camp, and Yogi Matto to the chumps.

There had been uneasy speculation about him for weeks, for the breaks had been many—and all bad. But men were afraid of him and said nothing. As though finding flavor in his tidings, he had accurately forecast each and every disaster, even to this storm which had kept the crowds away tonight. And, weirdly, he had forecast, again with relish, his own death.

Some had said he was a Russian, but then a Hindu had come out of the crowd and the two had spoken in the Hindu's tongue. And when they had dubbed him as being from India, they found that he spoke Chinese and Turkish as well. A razorback had once seen the insides of his trunks and had pronounced their heaviness occasioned by fully a hundred books of ancient aspect, filled with mysterious signs and incantations.

That the Professor did possess some remarkable power was apparent to all. For no matter how much anger might be vented against him for driving clients into hysteria with his evil forebodings of their future and thus hurting the show, no man had ever been able to approach those eyes.

No man, that is, but Little Tom Little.

Just how this was, even the Professor could not tell. But from the first, Little Tom Little, an ace at the heartless art of mimicry, had found humor in the Professor and had won laughter by mocking him. The matter had developed into nearly an open feud, but Little Tom Little, inwardly caring desperately what the world thought of him, but outwardly a swaggering satirist, had continued merrily.

The mockery always went well with the crowd, just as the Professor did not. Little Tom Little, in the sideshow, would get the crowd after the Professor was done and, very cunningly, would tell their fortunes in a doleful voice which made the tent billow from the resulting laughter. These crowds, sensing evil, had not liked to believe what the Professor had said.

And the gypsy camp had laughed with Little Tom Little, even though no man but he dared to affront the Professor.

The Professor had not forgotten his powerlessness to turn aside those quips. He had not forgotten that a man just thirty inches tall had held him up to ridicule for months. He had said nothing.

But he was dying now. And he was glad to die, secure as he was in a knowledge of the glories which awaited him elsewhere. In dying he would find himself at last. But he could not forget Little Tom Little. No! He would remember Little Tom Little with a legacy. He had already made out the paper.

Someone was coming up the aisle of the car, and then the doorknob rattled and Little Tom Little entered the stateroom. Water ran from his tiny poncho as he took it off.

The Professor moved a little on his pillow so that he could see his visitor, whose head was just above the height of the bunk.

Little Tom Little's handsome self, usually so gay, was now steeped in seriousness. He felt that he ought to feel highly sympathetic, and yet he could not understand exactly why, out of the whole crew, he had been sent for at this moment—for the physician outside had told him that the Professor could not last long. He was repelled, as always, by those filmed eyes, for Little Tom was not a brave man, for all his front. He waited for the Professor to speak.

"You are wondering," said the Professor, "why I have sent for you." His voice was very low and Little Tom had to put his ear close to the evil-smelling lips. "In your mind," said the Professor, "you are turning over the reasons for this. I must put you at ease, for I have always respected you."

Little Tom was startled.

"Yes," said the Professor, "I have seen much to admire in you. On the lot about me, men are afraid. They spread away from me when I approach. But you . . . you were brave, Tom Little. You did not cower away. You had steel enough in you not only to meet me and speak to me, but you also had courage enough to risk my wrath—a thing which all other men feared."

Little Tom had not considered that his mockery required so much nerve.

"It was not courage," he protested, trying to say something decent to a dying man. "You just imagined—"

"No, I did not imagine. Men slink from me for a peculiar

6

reason, Little Tom. They slink from me because I impel them. Yes, that is the truth. I force them away. I want nothing to do with men, for I loathe all mankind. I impelled them, Little Tom Little. Long before now you must have realized that I command strange and subtle arts beyond the understanding of these foolish and material slaves of their own desires."

Whatever Little Tom Little had expected to hear from a dying man, this certainly was far from it. In common with everyone, he had suspected these things, but he had been urged to derision instead of terror, not through understanding, but by nature.

"By such command," continued the Professor, "I am now able to leave this world for one far better, knowing exactly where I am going. But behind me I shall leave a little more than a corpse. I have a few things here—"

"Oh, you're not going to die!" said Little Tom Little.

"If I believed that, I should be very sad," replied the Professor. "But to return to why I brought you here; you must know that I was unable to make any impression upon you."

"Well . . . I never felt any."

"That is it," said the Professor. "I cannot touch you. And that means that you have it subconsciously in your power to handle and control all phases of the black arts."

"Me?"

"You. And I appreciate this. I respect you for it. I have a generous heart, Little Tom, for I am a learned man and can understand all things. Behind me I shall leave my books. They are ancient and rare, and most of them in mystic languages. But I have translated many of the passages into English.

7

These volumes contain the black lore of the ancient peoples of the East. Only a few men have any notion whatever of the depths of such wisdom, of the power to be gained through its use. And you, Little Tom, are to be my heir. The paper here is witnessed. I give it to you."

Little Tom took the sheet and glanced wonderingly from it to the Professor.

"You did not believe I was truly your friend," said the Professor. "Now, what greater proof is there than this legacy so freely given? Does that prove my good regard, Little Tom?"

"Why . . . yes. Sure."

"When I am dead, then, add my trunks to your own baggage. Study my volumes well. Can I give you any greater gift than wisdom?"

"I . . . I don't know what to say. This . . . this is so much—"

"Do not mention it, please. It is a little thing, for I shall need them no longer. Now go, for in the few minutes which remain to me I wish to concentrate all my powers upon the world which lies awaiting me."

Little Tom was still so astonished that he stumbled going to the door. Somehow he got into his poncho and fumbled up the aisle. After a little he found he still gripped the paper in his minute hand and put it away. He was upset to such an extent that he went down the train, not remembering to get off and seek his own car.

And so it was that he opened the door to Hermann Schmidt's private car and was halfway down it before he realized where he was. And then it was too late!

"You did not believe I was truly your friend," said the Professor. "Now, what greater proof is there than this legacy so freely given? Does that prove my good regard, Little Tom?"

Hermann Schmidt, as ringmaster and tacit governor of Johnson's Super Shows, was known to have the temper of a Prussian drill sergeant and, as a near giant, could afford to give it vent. He was sitting at a writing table, checking piles of currency into a capacious tin box. So pleasant did the task appear that not until the door—held for a time by the hydraulic shock absorber—closed did he realize that his sanctum sanctorum had been invaded.

Schmidt whirled like a bull suddenly stabbed from behind and came half to his feet, gripping the chair as though about to hurl it. But he looked in vain for a moment, for he instinctively searched a level about two feet over Little Tom's head, where a normal man's face would have been. And then he saw Little Tom who, in this crisis, was paralyzed by the ringmaster's terrible wrath, which seemed all out of proportion to so small a crime.

With a hair-singeing oath in German, Schmidt expressed both relief and rage. He lunged forward and grabbed Little Tom by the front of his poncho, lifting him bodily three feet off the floor as he might a sawdust doll.

"So! You are spying!"

And Little Tom was shaken so violently that he could not have answered even if Schmidt's grip and the resulting strain on the poncho were not choking him. Little Tom, even in this instant of terror, could not comprehend why Schmidt should be so mad.

"You think this is a runway! You come in! Maybe you think you own the show? Maybe you just bought it! Maybe Mrs. Johnson just to you gave it! A lesson you need, you tenth of a human being!"

And as though he was putting out a cat, he rushed to the vestibule, Little Tom dangling high, and with a final, ferocious shake, lifted him over the edge and let him fall the eight feet down into the mud.

Little Tom was stunned. He could hear Schmidt's voice, far away, bidding him to let himself be taught so to walk around the next time he came to this car.

Dimly he saw Schmidt up on the car platform, much as a drowning sailor might have seen the Colossus of Rhodes. Little Tom dazedly pried himself out of the mud. His shoulder was full of lightning and he could barely support even his meager weight upon his twisted ankle. In him a rage was kindled, to run along like a dot of fire eating the length of a fuse. A fuse which was to burn for weeks ere it reached the dynamite.

If I have to be a midget another minute," cried Little Tom Little, "I'll—I'll use a stretcher on myself!"

And indeed he sounded very desperate, sitting there on his stage in the heat of the newly deserted tent. Somewhere at hand the circus band was oompahing in preparation for the entrance of Gordon—"the wuruld's gr-r-r-atest wil' animal trainah who performs the suicidal feat of putting through their paces ta-wenty feerocious tigahs from Bengal and ta-wenty man-eating lions, all at one and the same time. Ladees and gennulmun—"

Little Tom Little winced as the faraway spiel reached him. How he hated cats!

Maizie was putting away their paraphernalia and looking

sad. Only an inch taller than Little Tom Little, she felt that his recriminations against his own lot somehow damned hers. And then, too, he was handsome and he had wit, and tiny though he was, there existed no better showman in the gypsy camp than himself.

"I'm sick of it!" said Little Tom with even greater emphasis.

"But why?" said Maizie, shutting down the lid of the small trunk and making things ready for the next act. "You're a genius, Tommy. Of all the sideshows, yours and mine draws best. You know how to keep them—"

"Keep them!" shouted Tommy, leaping up to all his thirty inches of height. "Who wants to keep them? Who wants to stand up here day after day with them packed up against this stage, rubbering and giggling and sweating and saying, 'Ain't he cute, Joe?' 'Ain't she the dearest thing, Martha?' Why do they like us? I'll tell you why. Because we're freaks! It isn't because we're good. It isn't because I give them a show. I'm a freak, see? A *freak*!"

The outburst subsided and he sank back into the small chair. Some of the other attractions glanced toward him from their remote platforms. Maizie patted his shoulder consolingly.

"Tommy, it's better to be the best midget star in the world than a failure as a big person."

"It's not! I'd rather dig ditches, if I could stand up and look my fellow man in the eye instead of examining his shins!"

"But, Tommy, that's senseless! No matter how hard you wish it, it will never come true. You're a midget and a very handsome one, and you're an artist—"

"How do I *know* I'm an artist? No matter how I work my act, I'll never know that. I'm 'cute' and 'darling' and— *Ugh!*"

"Tommy, if you want to leave the show—"

"No! Who's talking about leaving the show? I know this business. And not all the Schmidts in the world can drive me away!"

"Has he done something to you lately?" said Maizie.

"Him? It's not what he *does*, it's what he doesn't do. There he is, the ringmaster! And do you think he'll ever notice a midget? I've tried to ask him for a spot in the big top, and time after time he's almost walked me down. If I were a big person—" He clenched his small fists bitterly. "He thinks he is a showman. Why, for all the brass in his voice, I could make a fool out of him in ten minutes in his own ring! Someday . . . someday I'm going to look up the Boss and I'm going to say, 'Mrs. Johnson, I want to be your ringmaster—'"

"So that's it again!" said Maizie. "Tommy, you know that will never be."

"Why not?" said Tommy darkly. "The ringmaster runs the show, and I'm tired of being a freak. You wait, Maizie! One of these days I'll *be* the ringmaster!"

"Tommy—"

"What's the matter now?"

"Tommy, you haven't been reading those books again, have you?"

"What books?"

"Tommy, don't be that way with me. When the Professor left you his trunks, he didn't like you any better than he ever had."

13

"What of that? Can't a man repent on his deathbed?"

"Yes, Tommy—but *did* he?"

"Look, let's not go into that."

"He hated you, Tommy. When you used to mimic his mitt reading, I could see him watching. He didn't think it was funny. It may be all right with anyone else in the show for you to take off their routine, but it never was with the Professor."

"Aw, you've been dreaming again! He did leave me his trunks, didn't he?"

"There's such a thing as vengeance after death, Tommy."

"Sure, but I haven't met his ghost yet."

"Not his ghost, Tommy. It's those books!"

Late that night Maizie lay wide awake and apparently sound asleep in the dark of the stateroom berth, fearfully watching Tommy, the king of midget showmen—who did not want his crown—sitting gnomelike at the dressing table, surrounded by a litter of cracked and weighty tomes whose parchment pages were like mummies' skin in the gloom. The book he was studying was so unwieldy that he had propped it with greasepaint cans to save his arms.

Maizie wanted badly to weep, to cry out, to plead with him and tell him how much he meant to her, but she lay like some perfect doll, put away and forgotten by a careless child.

She had been with him for five years on the sawdust trail, and each day she found something new about him. The world pushed so heavily against him, and his tiny body was so frail and his spirit so great that she would have given her very heart to have been a big person and able to defend him.

14

To the world of superlative polysyllables and sawdust, Little Tom Little was known for an ace. As a half-pint Punchinello who dared to deride them all, he had gained much fame. None of them knew that the dapper, vest-pocket edition longed for anything but to keep his name properly on the posters. Had they known, they probably would have laughed at him about it. And they would have howled over his ambition to be a ringmaster. But only Maizie knew. Only Maizie had seen him in a deserted tent cracking a long whip around his tiny black boots and putting imaginary rosinbacks through their paces. And Maizie—all was not well with Tommy and so nothing was well with her.

A big cat was howling his displeasure somewhere along the train and Maizie saw Little Tom Little fidget uneasily. How he had hated the big fellows since that break in Kansas City when the lion had almost killed him! And seeing him wince at the sound, Maizie felt willing to go and gag the animal, if it would give Tommy a little rest.

What would he dig from those volumes? The danger of a cat was as nothing to the knowledge he so eagerly gulped.

Everyone had known the Professor as a misfit, and more than one had breathed a sigh of relief when he had passed into what he had described as a glowing land of happiness. But wherever he had gone, he had left evil memories behind him. He had been a vulture of bad omen, a cadaver without a coffin, a man whose eyes gleamed at the tidings of misfortune. He had lived on bad luck, had purveyed ominous forebodings to cringing clients, and his lot had not been easy. He had been far more than a sideshow mitt reader. And when Tommy, impartial as always, had taken to giving a mimic mitt act to take off the Professor, Maizie had known that someday Tommy would pay for humbling a vicious pride. Tommy's act had been funny. But now—

Why had the Professor left those books, his entire library, to *Tommy?*

The big cat roared more loudly and Tommy impatiently leaped up to wrestle the window down. Reaching thus across Maizie, he saw that she did not sleep.

"Anything wrong?" said Tommy.

She saw how abstracted he was. "Nothing."

"You feel all right, don't you?"

"Yes. Certainly!"

Tommy kissed her thoughtlessly and went back to his book. She saw how animated he was, how his small body could scarcely contain the enthusiasm he built up within it.

And when he turned, his face flushed, and cried, "Maizie! I've got it!" it was all she could do to repress a sob of despair. As gaily as she could, she answered, "What is it, Tommy?"

"The solution! I said today I was never again going to be a midget. Well! I'm not! Tomorrow . . . tomorrow I shall be ringmaster of this show!"

Her alarm was real, but she masked it. "How . . . how do you mean, Tommy?"

"Why, it's here. It's all here! This is a treatise on the transmigration of the soul. You understand that, don't you? When a fellow kicks off, he enters into another body, see? It's a wonder I never found this before. It's all marked and there was a slip of paper between the pages. Say, maybe the

Professor wasn't such a bad egg after all, huh? He said when he left me all these that he'd indicated one place specially, and this must be it."

"Oh, Tommy," she whispered. "Are you sure it won't mean—"

But Tommy's excited voice swept on and his thirty inches of height seemed to double themselves already. "It says if the transmigration of the soul can be effected after death, it is logical to conclude that it can be done in life. It says the only vital, thinking portion of man is his soul energy, and that it can be projected from one body to another. Maizie, think what this means!"

She took heart, for he seemed to have nothing definite. But Tommy sent her faint hopes tumbling.

"And here's how it's done! How simple! All you have to do is miss a few meals, say breakfast and lunch, and then begin your concentration upon the object into which you desire to transfer. Think of it, Maizie! To leave your body and become another person! To put behind you everything you have done wrong, and all the mistakes you have made, and begin all over in a different guise!"

"What . . . what happens to the other person?"

But he swept this away as well. "Why, naturally, whether he will or no, he is forced to occupy the body you have left—or else die."

"Tommy . . . this is dangerous!" But she could not say more, for the possibilities of this terrible idea were overwhelming.

"And it's so easy! It says here that man becomes everything he senses, even for the briefest of instants. If you look at a hero in a story, you are, for the duration of that story, the

17

hero. You take on his mannerisms and his way of speech. But because he is just a hero of a story he cannot return that concentration. It says that all men, when talking to other men, are too watchful of the other's words and actions and too conscious of self to achieve this feat. But if one refuses to be aware of the possible menace to self from the other ego, then it is simple to completely assimilate the other person and to project oneself into the other.

"Think of it, Maizie! If I needed money!"

"Tommy, Tommy, this is madness! It cannot possibly work!"

"Look, Maizie. I have not eaten since noon, and it is now nearing midnight—"

"What are you going to do?"

"Maizie, look at me."

"No!"

"Maizie, do you love me?"

"Oh, Tommy . . ."

And then she felt a curious chill, a feeling as though she had risen several feet above herself and now hung suspended over her body in the air. But in a moment she was again in the bed.

"It . . . it takes practice," said Tommy, beads of sweat upon his brow. "Look at me, Maizie!"

"Please! Tommy, for the love of the God that made us . . . !"

And again she felt that chill, that feeling of lift. Terror struck at her lest she were blind and deaf.

But in a moment she could begin to see a little and hear the big cat snarling far off. With a start she found herself gazing, not at the dressing table from the bed, but at the bed from the dressing table! The big book was heavy against her hand. The curtain of the bed moved, as though blown by a gentle breeze.

She saw "Maizie" sit up in the berth!

Dazedly she looked at herself, turned her attention to the body which she now inhabited, not believing the trousers with their tight belt or the tie and collar which choked her. She whirled to the mirror and recoiled at the image of Tommy!

Tommy was shaken to the last spark of his consciousness. He was propped up on one elbow, staring in disbelief at the nightdress which he clutched. He came to himself and whipped a hand to his head. The long, golden curls—

They stared at each other, then, silent and numb with awe. When minutes had passed, Tommy laughed shakily. "You see—it works."

"But . . . but Tommy . . . how are we going to get back?"

But he was triumphant now and growing bolder. "Why should we?" he teased.

"It's . . . it's horrible, Tommy!" And she was hard put to keep back her tears. "Undo this . . . this terrible spell! Please, Tommy!"

The longing to be herself made her sight dim. There was a whirling motion about her and she went blind and feelingless, and then she was shivering, as herself, in the middle of the stateroom, looking at Tommy once more.

Suddenly she threw herself at his feet, trying hard to find the words to tell him that this thing could bring nothing but unhappiness.

Tommy hardly noticed her in his excitement. "These are

19

the right words to think, then. These words written here! It's true! These years of misery are done! No more do I have to step quickly from the path of the big people and look a man in his shins. Eye to eye, Maizie! And tomorrow"—he lowered his voice to a whisper—"tomorrow I shall be ringmaster!"

Hermann Schmidt arose and dressed with his usual extreme care. His boots had been polished into black mirrors; his stock had been starched into armor plate; his waistcoat had been brushed until it resembled newly shed blood. He set his swallow-tailed coat to perfection upon his mighty shoulders and then, inventorying himself in the mirror, petted his gleaming top hat down upon his broad brow. He selected a crop from a rack, glanced at his watch, and sauntered down the cars to the special diner. As he went, everyone from razorback to high traps bowed low and, in return, Schmidt gave them lofty nods which held a certain amount of doubt, as though he was not quite sure they existed.

Such was his show day routine. Mighty and domineering, a colossus of size and influence, it was small wonder that the fate of the show rested so certainly in his hands—for who, looking at such a figure of a man, could doubt his ability?

He could not remember a time when he had not been a man of importance. As a boy, he had been his father's son and his father had been a ringmaster in the old country. And why shouldn't a man be important, if he knew the business from bale ring to stakes?

He ended his individual spec at the snowy cloth of his breakfast table whereon was spread the local morning paper.

He disdained such yokel print and sat looking through the
car window at the less fortunate denizens of sawdust who
trailed toward the crumb castle of the grounds dressed to
kick 'em by ten o'clock. Far away, somebody tuned up a horse
piano, and nearby a bull man sicced his rubber mules upon
a mired wagon amid much trumpeting and shouting. It was
altogether soothing, and Schmidt sighed comfortably.

Fried potatoes and a small steak were placed under his
nose by an obsequious man and Schmidt armed himself and
prepared to attack.

He became conscious of someone who had slid into the seat
across the table. He knew who it was and repressed a shudder.
Ruefully he stared at the silver service, which reflected a
face in all manner of distortions. The face was ancient and
seamed and sallow, and the eyes held an expression which
made Schmidt wince; for, certain as he was of most things,
he doubted whether he could keep on forever avoiding the
necessity of fixing a date for their marriage.

"Good morning, Mrs. Johnson," he said with a low bow.

She smiled in a fluttery way. "How are you today, darling?"

"Very fine, thank you, Mrs. Johnson."

"Hermann"—she reached out a ruin of a hand and touched
the back of his own—"must we be so formal? After all, we
are engaged."

"Forgive me, my lovely one," he said, "but I was so engrossed
with affairs—" Then inspiration struck: "Unless we can show
a profit on our balance sheets, we mustn't think of our own
private affairs. For I promise I shall never marry you until I
can prove my full worth."

"But we are doing such good business—"

"Prices are up everywhere," he reminded her. "Our feed bill alone is enough to ruin us. And our licenses have doubled, what with sales taxes and all. *Ach,* my darling, it is not good. But with me—I repeat my vow. I shall make a profit, before we are man and wife."

"Oh, Hermann—you are so noble."

Hermann smiled in a somewhat sickly fashion and again addressed his steak. She had been such a lovely woman once, he thought. Too bad she had not been able to keep the years from rolling over her. She was active—indeed, it was said she could outride any rosinback in the show. But that was hardly compensation. He wished desperately for a moment that he had never thought up the idea of proposing to her, but still—he could hold her off a little longer, with skill. And when the final time came, he would leave a note. How she would squirm when she read it! It was his one consoling thought in an otherwise revolting association.

He patted her hand in hypocritical affection as he stood up. "Never mind, my dear. Just leave all this to me, and we'll show a profit yet."

"If I didn't have you, Hermann . . ."

Hurriedly he sought the morning outside the car. He stood for a moment, mantling himself with majesty, and then strode through the piles of gear toward the grounds. Ahead of him the tail end of the march was filing into the street to the brassy tune of the steam fiddle and the cloppety-clop of horses' hoofs. The grounds were deserted save for razorbacks, lot lice, a few spielers and menagerie men. These nodded politely but, since they were not worth notice, Schmidt swept by.

With the air of a king entering his palace, he climbed into the wagon which would ordinarily be the governor's office, but which only he occupied. Easing into a seat at the desk, he unlocked the safe at its side and drew out the books.

For the next half-hour he made the art of the show's slip artists seem pale, and as he worked a stiff smile of lofty satisfaction came upon his face. It went away swiftly when there sounded a knock. He threw the books into the safe and slammed the door.

A very beautiful girl timidly entered at his call. She had great, soft eyes and long blond curls, and the loveliness of her figure belied its trained strength.

"Betty!" he said, pulling out a chair.

"I didn't come to . . . to sit down," she replied.

But nevertheless he eased her into the seat. Resentfully but scared, she sat on the chair's edge, staring at him.

There was triumph in his voice. "I knew, sooner or later, that you'd come to me of your own accord. After all, it isn't fitting that I should always be the one to arrange meetings."

"I came," she said in a strained tone, "to tell you that this . . . this wild plan of yours can't go on."

"Nonsense! You have been thinking too much. Don't we love each other? Can't—"

"No!" she cried out. "Don't say that, Hermann. You haven't any right. I have never told you I loved you."

"It is enough," he smiled, "that I love you. And my plans

23

are your plans. Before long we will leave this show. You shall divorce Gordon and marry me. We'll be rich, and you shall be more famous than you have ever dreamed."

"It's all crazy," said Betty, trying to withstand the onslaught of his personality. "I've been trying to think straight about this. And . . . I still love Gordon, Hermann. He may be rough and forgetful—"

"There was a day," said Hermann, "when you two had small enough spots."

"That was a long time ago. I've worked hard to become an ace. I'm one of your stars! I work hard!"

"True, you were fortunate in having Gillman kill himself. But of course, if you insist that you will not go with me, you and Gordon can, of course, go together. And the big cats can stay with me, for there's a matter of feed bills for them. And there are many wire acts I can get. There's a telegram here somewhere"—and he made a pretense of searching for it—"from Thomas and Maletto, wondering if I could place them. Their high wire—"

"Hire them, then!" she cried. "I can't go on, Hermann. Give us back our contracts—"

Hermann laughed sharply. "I picked you both out of the mud and taught you everything you know—and you talk to me this way! But there's one thing you've forgotten. Jerry Gordon is happy just so long as he is playing games with his beloved big cats. He was ruined once. You know what he did—he blamed you for everything and lushed all the liquor in sight. And he'd have killed you with abuse if I hadn't yanked you up out of nothing, to star him with his cats and you on the high wire."

"He . . . he didn't mean to be so bad to me. He's a good man, Hermann. He fights forty big cats all together in the arena and there isn't another man in the business who can do that. And I have a high wire without a net, and the customers—"

"Without my consent, you and Gordon are nothing. Without his act he'll drop even lower than he was when I picked you up and starred you both. It would probably kill him, Betty. And you as well."

"But he loves me, Hermann! What's past is past! It's useless to think of running away with you and divorcing him. Crazy!"

"And yet if you don't," said Hermann, smiling, "you'll very much wish you had."

The strain of holding out so long against his will at last broke her own. She began to weep quietly and forlornly, and when at last he cupped her face in his hands and said, "Of course you'll go with me, won't you?" she could only nod a weary assent.

And, leaving his wagon after she had gone, Hermann Schmidt appeared a match for more than a dozen mere lion trainers. An aloof demigod, secure in his realm, proud of his abilities and cunning, he passed the sideshow—with no eyes at all for the midget who stood there, apparently waiting for someone.

Little Tom Little was so filled with excitement that he found great difficulty in breathing. To him, Schmidt was a Brobdingnagian, a Zeus and a Colossus of Rhodes all superadded into one, and when, in this breath before the zero minute, he contemplated what he was about to do, he was flabbergasted by his own temerity.

Certain he was that Schmidt knew all about it and was about to break his crop on Tommy's small skull. For there he came, as though riding the Juggernaut car, gigantic and unstoppable, the science of black magic to the contrary.

But so fascinated had Tommy been since the instant of conceiving this bold plan that any passing doubt was drowned in a torrent of enthusiasm.

He must time this to the split instant. He must not forget those words which seared his brain.

Eagerly he sought Schmidt's eye.

Proud to bursting of both his height and bearing, Schmidt was unable to brook even a glimpse of a midget. But eyes are traitorous things which follow anything that moves or sparkles, and as a last resort, Tommy had armed himself with a small silver whip. He swooshed it viciously through the air. Schmidt glanced that way, instantly revolted by the midget's image.

To a razorback who stood languidly by, what followed was not particularly startling, not even to be suspected. For Schmidt merely stopped where he was and appeared to be offended, which was not unusual. Little Tom Little was apparently eagerly seeking to say something to the ringmaster. But the two did not exchange a word. The midget's mouth moved as though he talked to himself, and Schmidt looked popeyed at such effrontery and, immediately after, somewhat blank. This was the only thing that the razorback remarked. Schmidt had never looked anything but severe in all circus knowledge. But after an instant of this, Schmidt—getting a grip on himself, it seemed—glanced down to take delighted inventory of his dress. And Little Tom Little, so it appeared, was nothing but disturbed by his own garb. Thereupon Schmidt, swinging his crop and again in a grandiose humor, strolled on his way, and the midget, starting to run after, noticed the razorback and moved wonderingly into the shadow of the deserted sideshow tent. . . .

After the first shock of the transition was over, Little Tom Little felt very much like a bean in a bass drum. When he took a step, he went about four times as far as he thought he should have gone, a fact which occasioned his stumbling over a guy rope and almost losing his dignity in the lap of Matilda, the World's Fattest Woman. He bowed with great difficulty and again misgauged his distance, almost knocking out his brains against a wagon side, so much further had he gone than he had expected.

Feeling embarrassed, he made off. Every day for years he had seen Matilda, and always she had reserved a large smile for him and perhaps some cookies—quite as though she mistook him for a mischievous little boy. And though always he had resented being looked on as a boy, he had never failed to enjoy either the cookies or the smile. But now Matilda looked sober and alarmed, and she had not spoken a word.

It was uncomfortable to feel, suddenly, that he was outside

the scope of her kindness. And when he came to consider it, he realized that people were not unkind to him—had never been truly unkind to Little Tom Little.

Well! He was not Little Tom Little anymore. He was Hermann Schmidt, the World's Greatest Ringmaster, Lord and Master of Johnson's Super Shows. And what if he did underestimate the length of his step and knock his hat against things he had always found far above him—he would get used to that! And what of Schmidt himself? Tommy had always been insanely jealous of that man's lofty position. Let Schmidt find out how the world looked from a midget's eye, and mend his ways accordingly!

Having kicked 'em, the troupers were streaming back from town, sweaty and cross and hungry, anxious to get rested before the afternoon show.

Standing in the entrance of the big top, Tommy—as Schmidt—watched them pass. Because he knew that Schmidt always did so, he assumed a somewhat critical air and bowed very seldom. It came to him with a slight shock that the people did not fall over themselves to notice him, and when they did, there were scowls.

It was a jarring experience to the ex-midget to be scowled upon, for in all his trouping he had never had anything but smiles for greeting.

Well, a fellow had to sacrifice something for his position, didn't he?

And yet there was an empty feeling in his soul, and a growing fright that maybe the world suspected something.

Had Maizie talked?

Had the Professor boasted before his death?

But no, these frowns were not accusative. These people thought they looked upon Hermann Schmidt, Ringmaster. They scowled because they were tired, that was all.

Jerry Gordon, riding in a wagon with Old Bab, his pet lion, had removed his sun hat to swab at its band when he caught sight of Schmidt. His scowl was deeper, and so filled with suspicion that Tommy was frightened. Gordon had always been the midget's friend, for all Tommy's hatred of cats. The question was, what did Gordon know? Why did he stop wiping out his hat and frown so heavily that he forgot what his hands were doing?

Tommy wished he had taken station anywhere but here. He felt that these people were looking straight through Schmidt—the body of Schmidt—and seeing Little Tom Little, and were all ready to fall upon him en masse and eat him up.

Betty, the high-wire artist, riding a bull's howdy, looked strangely at Schmidt as she went by. There was some kind of warning, though a reluctant one, in her expression. And Little Tom Little, who had always secretly adored and respected both the girl and her skill, read some distaste in her glance as well. Plainly, though, she was trying to give him a message, and a disquieting one at that.

It was all a puzzle to the ex-midget but, overestimating his stride in an attempt to compensate, he again discovered his size and appearance and took heart.

What the devil! Wasn't he Schmidt, the great Schmidt?

Ringmaster of the Johnson Super Shows? Yes! No longer a midget, small enough to be trod under every foot, but a big person, and one of the greatest ringmasters in the world! They were afraid of Schmidt, that was it. Schmidt was their master, and now . . . now, ah! Wasn't *he* Schmidt?

Crossing the lot, he heard a voice call, "Hermann!" in sweet accents. It was repeated several times, for he was not yet used to the name. Finally he realized that the call was for himself and he turned with a mimicry of Schmidt's reserved air.

Mrs. Johnson had always been ready to laugh at Little Tom Little's jokes, and now, when he saw her regarding him from her tent entrance with a very much different manner, he had to recollect himself very fast to keep from being startled. As yet he had not had to speak to anyone, and he was frightened at the prospect, lest his somewhat midgetish voice would betray him. With a guilty manner altogether quite foreign to the true Schmidt, he approached her.

Additional dismay came over him when he found that he was expected to make the opening remark. He recollected himself and twirled his mustache as he had seen Schmidt do so often, his eyes on the sky.

"I think," he said with careful judging, "that we will have a very fine crowd today."

"Hermann—"

Tommy was alarmed now. "And the acts seem to be in fine shape. I guess if every show we had was as promising as this one, we'd all be rich in no time."

There came a change in her aged face and he welcomed

it. "Things have been like this for the whole season without our getting anything but poorer. Have you some good news of some sort?"

"Ah . . . well . . . you never can tell," he said vaguely.

"You're holding something back!" said Mrs. Johnson with a kittenish air which accused him of teasing her.

Tommy regretted he had brought the matter to the front. "No. Honest, I didn't mean anything. It's just going to be a good day, I guess. Maybe," he added brightly, "maybe I better be getting over to the big top to make sure everything is going all right."

She looked startled, but he moved away too fast to be stopped.

"Hmm," said Mrs. Johnson suspiciously.

Tommy felt unsettled. He ran a clammy hand over the unaccustomed bushiness of his physiognomy. In the protection of a snack stand, he seated himself upon a box and tried to collect his thoughts. The things he had begun to find out about Hermann Schmidt were not at all quieting, and though he had already begun to regret his swap, there was still too much glamour in the thought of being a ringmaster not to give the thing a thorough try. After all, he could last long enough to crack his whip in the main event, and after that he could let fate take its course.

Mealtime had robbed the lot of its attendants for the moment and so he sat on, waiting for something else to happen. For thought food, he used the fact that the attendants had been getting thin. That had been news, for pay had been regular enough. It amused him the next moment to think that he—Schmidt—would be the one to know the most about such affairs.

Presently the lot began to be popular once more and, feeling conspicuous, he started to move off, wondering where he should go, until it occurred to him that the white wagon, after all, was his. However, his few minutes of rest had spotted him, and promptly he was surrounded by men who had problems to be solved.

Although he had the routine of sawdust land at his fingertips, it made him very uncomfortable to be called upon for so many decisions at once. Joe Middler was taking too much "strawberry shortcake." His shill wasn't getting a long enough string of coconuts. The pup opera was minus its canine star, who had wandered too near a gravedigger's cage, and it was either a new mutt or a dead hyena. The payoff was too high on a juice joint, and if John Law objected to the kife, what else could a guy do but howl? A kinker had a twisted wrist, and he figured Bill had had it in for 'im anyway since that dame in St. Looie had shown good sense, and he wasn't goin' to get a broken neck over any fool dame!

Tommy dispensed justice as best he could, and twice he turned down out-and-out bribes for a decision, much to the astonishment of the would-be bribers.

When things were at last settled and the show was in order, spots had begun and the place was humming with thistle chins. The spielers were clowning the come-in to what appeared to be a great crowd. People from far and near were already milling near the marquee and, all in all, it was a bright, hot, sweaty, dusty circus day, with bawling barkers all snarled up with the yelping horse piano and the jig band, and the constant hum of pleased suckers, with an undertone of lions' roars and clacking wheels.

Tommy felt better. This was his element, and of this element he was now king. So delighted was he at the thought of at last snapping the lash in the hoople to the admiration of all, that he quite forgot to think at all of what was happening to himself, erstwhile Little Tommy Little, now Hermann Schmidt—in the flesh at least.

But Schmidt had not forgotten anything, even in the soul-shattering experience of all of a sudden watching himself flick his crop and walk away, leaving behind a man less than thirty inches high.

Schmidt's first impulse had been to dash after himself, crying out for help. But his coldly logical brain had told him that he would look very silly doing so. For Schmidt, as always, had sized up the situation as a purely abstract problem and was determined to solve it the best he could.

In the dusty emptiness of the sideshow tent, he had brought himself into a full realization of his strange and very disturbing predicament. In the Black Forest of his native land, he had heard such things had happened and, so far as he could tell, no kind fate had come along immediately to undo them. And the longer he measured his slightness up against his surroundings, the more he became convinced of the awfulness of his situation and the need to do something about it.

Schmidt recognized clearly that this extraordinary situation

33

might well lead to an exposition of his former self. Therefore it behooved him, as soon as possible, to obtain the neat cache he had made and wipe out all existing records and letters now in his safe. This done, he would be less apprehensive and could, if necessary, grab a red light and be gone, though now merely a midget, with his gains, leaving the usurper of his true body to face the music.

There was only one disadvantage to this, and that lay with the person who had stolen his identity, for that person now had the only keys to the white wagon. However, his sudden smallness had not deflated Schmidt's courage. He would wait for the usurper, attempt to get the keys. Failing that, he would carry out the rest of his plan.

And so it came about that when Little Tom Little betook his Schmidtly self up the steps of the white wagon and inserted a key in the lock, he was not the only one who entered.

As the midget slammed shut the door behind them, Tommy leaped a foot, whirling. From Schmidt's malevolent expression, it was plain that something horrible was about to happen.

"You," said Schmidt, in his now piping midget voice, "are going to do something about this!"

Tommy momentarily forgot his stature. Not unlike a midget, he had never been very long on courage when it came to physical conflict, but so engrossed was he with his determination to direct the show, if only once, that he made a stern show of it.

"Why should I?" he said, flicking his great black boots with his riding crop and staring down at the midget Schmidt.

"I don't know the game," snarled Schmidt, "but you won't

live long enough to get anything on me!" And, so saying, he made a sudden motion at a drawer and Tommy found himself staring at a very large gun in a very steady hand. For an instant he was very nervous.

Then, "Go ahead and shoot. This is *your* body—if you want to mess it up that's okay with me."

Uncertainly the gun wavered down, inch by inch. Schmidt was comparing their respective statures while he racked his brain for some means to outwit Tommy and overcome him.

Before Schmidt could assert himself again, there came a sharp rap on the door. Schmidt made as though to open it, recollected himself and stood back. In the blank darkness of failure, he could think of only one course: to throw open the safe and snatch up the file cases. Cramming his pockets full of letters and notebooks, he backed hastily into the lavatory.

The impatient rapping continued and the knob was rattled. Without understanding what Schmidt was trying to get away with, for there certainly was no egress from the lavatory, Tommy heeded the anxiety of those knocks.

Betty flung herself into the room. Her face alternately burned and went cold with the intensity of her emotion. She stood against the closed door, as though blocking another out.

"Hermann," she cried, "he's coming! He saw me leave here this morning and he's on his way now! He'll tear this place apart!"

"Who?" said Tommy blankly.

"My husband! Hermann, for the love of heaven, don't stand there staring! Give me my letters and let me go! My letters, do you hear? He'll *find* them!"

Tommy looked dazedly at the lovely girl and then at the gutted safe. In the forward compartment of the wagon, Schmidt evidently had the required epistles. And because he had only a faint glimmering of what this was about, Tommy made no move to open the lavatory door until it was too late.

Another had entered the wagon.

Like a thundercloud which blankets the land in darkness, Mrs. Johnson dimmed the wagon. There was no hurry to her movements, only vengeful promise. She looked the terrified girl over from the toes of her slippers to the tip of her tinsel crown—and then, with curling lip, she took in the man she thought was Schmidt.

"If I interrupt your tryst," said the governor acidly, "forgive me."

"No, no!" cried Betty. "You don't understand!"

"I am afraid that I do—entirely too well. This accounts for many things! At least *some* of my people are faithful to me. When they told me that you had come here, I did not want to believe. But now that I see it with my own eyes—"

Betty was staring wildly past her across the lot. She made an unsuccessful attempt to get by the older woman, but was thrown back.

"Let me go!" Betty moaned. "You don't understand! He'll kill me if he finds me here!"

"And quite fitting, too!" said Mrs. Johnson. "I shall make certain that I see it. Schmidt, you have five minutes to pack and leave this lot. And if you ever try to get a job with another circus, you'll find that I am still respected in the business—if not by you, then by other companies."

"Wait!" cried Tommy, all befuddled. "What's happened? What have I done?"

The old harridan bared her teeth and perhaps would have made a scorching answer, had not she been thrust aside.

The only sound in the stillness was spots in the big top, for the show had already begun. And that gay blatting of brass was much out of place in this atmosphere of murder.

Jerry Gordon's bronzed chest heaved and his great muscles corded and uncorded as he gripped his blank gun and his whip. In his eyes was the look of his own cats intent upon a kill.

Betty threw herself upon him with a sharp cry. "Jerry! Jerry, you don't understand!"

He spurned her with his boot, never taking his eyes off the man he took for Schmidt.

Tommy had begun to sweat. In all his career he had stood undaunted before crowds, had given vent to mockery and sarcasm without stint. But at the slightest threat of physical pain, he had always shrunk away. And now, forgetting his own strength, forgetting that he was no longer thirty inches tall, he backed hastily away from the anger which blasted him.

Jerry Gordon moved ahead, cold intent plain in his every move.

At the door a man yelled, "Hey, Mrs. Johnson!" But the suspense in the room was too much for her to forsake it even with a glance.

"Mrs. Johnson!" cried another voice outside.

Impatiently she looked around at the clamor and saw two stakers who, between them, held a midget helpless in their strong grasps.

"We found 'im droppin' out of a back window," said a staker. "You said to watch this place, and this guy's got a mitt fulla dough!"

Tommy, as Schmidt, was not paying much heed to what they were saying. All he saw was Jerry Gordon advancing with the full intention of making hamburger out of him, and there on the steps his own true self, wholly unmenaced by a whip, gun and brawn.

It was so automatic that he hardly had to think to do it. Just *zip!* and it was over. Tommy was standing on the steps, once more thirty inches tall, looking with keen relief upon an astounded Schmidt being advanced upon by Jerry Gordon. Let Schmidt get out of his own messes as best he could! Let him be expelled from the camp! To the devil with being a ringmaster, anyhow!

Gordon raised his whip and brought it sizzling down. It seemed inevitable that it would take the ringmaster's head from his shoulders. But no! Up came the crop to fend, and out shot a cannonball fist to knock Gordon almost out of the white wagon.

Gordon, staggering, again prepared to leap into the fray. But Schmidt roared, "Stand where you are, you fool! You've made enough mistakes for one day!"

"When I've done with you," cried Gordon, "we'll see who was right!"

"Right!" bellowed Schmidt in icy rage. "Tell me what you think is wrong!"

"You know already," snapped Gordon.

"If I did, would I ask you?"

"You devil!" cried Gordon. "You steal my wife and then you've got the gall to throw it in my teeth!"

He started to attack once more. And once more Schmidt's brute force stopped him, held him in a vise.

"Your wife? Why, you idiot, what would I have to do with your wife? If a performer cannot transact business with me in my office without a foolish has-been trailing around for 'vengeance,' then the business has changed—changed more than I want to see it. Bah, you simpleton! She knows that you are failing. She knows that I contemplated throwing out your act in midseason, contract or no contract. And she came to plead for you. She came to beg me not to break your heart. And because she humbles herself for the likes of you, you are willing to debase her character before all these people, to accuse her of vileness which never could have occurred in her lovely head! And you call yourself a man, Gordon? You have the nerve to stand before us after that, Gordon? Apologize to Betty, or I'll have your heart!"

Bewildered, Gordon turned to his wife, but he could read nothing from her tear-stained face but shame, and that he read wrong.

"Forgive me . . . Betty," he said.

"There's a show going on," said Schmidt, "in case you have failed to notice it. For the moment, Gordon, we'll retain you despite your cesspool suspicions. And because, Mrs. Johnson, you could not run this show at all were it not for me, I'll accept your apologies and condescend to stay on, at least until you can find another ringmaster and manager. Now clear out while I straighten myself up. Bah, what fools you are!"

Betty and Gordon sought to leave. Mrs. Johnson, feeling very much ashamed of herself, wrung her hands. "Hermann—"

"Yes!" gruffly.

"Hermann . . . can you forgive me?"

"We'll talk of that later. Clear out and let me change!"

But the group on the steps stood firm. The two stakers were too single-track of mind not to remember that they held a captive. Mrs. Johnson backed into them, and almost stepped on Tommy.

"What we gonna do with this guy?" begged a staker. "He's got his mitts full of dough, and we caught him comin' outa the back windows."

Schmidt pushed them back from Tommy and stood there on a higher step, looking amusedly down at the midget. But the amusement in his eyes was of an awful kind, and Tommy shuddered.

Schmidt yanked the filing cases out of Tommy's hands. "The day's take," said Schmidt, looking meaningly at Mrs. Johnson. "That back window is always open. It would not admit a grown man, but it would certainly let in a midget. I think we have here," he said with satisfaction, "the reason why we have been losing money with such regularity."

"Wh-What?" gasped Tommy. "Why . . . you know you—"

"Go ahead," said Schmidt. "Lie out of it if you can!" He looked again at Mrs. Johnson as though to say, "Wait till you hear *this*!"

But all Tommy said was "*Ulp*."

"Tommy," said Mrs. Johnson. "I can't . . . can't believe that *you*—"

"There's the evidence," said Schmidt. "Listen, you two," he ordered the stakers, "take this fellow into the pad room and hold him until after the show. We'll get John Law to look out for him, after that."

Tommy swallowed hard and felt tears of rage welling up. But what could he do? He was the only one who had any true knowledge of Schmidt's defections.

But wait! Schmidt had averted disaster only for the moment; what a trick to change around again!

Tommy bent a calculating eye upon the ringmaster up there in the entrance of the white wagon. The second Schmidt spoke to him again, Schmidt was done!

At the moment, however, Schmidt had other objects of interest and, horror of horrors, it was another who spoke to Tommy.

"I'm sorry about this, kid. I didn't think—"

It happened so fast that Tommy could not prevent it. There was a swish and a shudder, and then Tommy was standing, whip in hand, looking at a helpless midget held fast between two brawny stakers!

This time, however, the transfer did not work with smoothness on the other's part. For Gordon appeared to be out on his feet, midget as he now was. He couldn't even focus his eyes, much less cry out.

And though Tommy did wait for that protest to be made so as to take full advantage of it and swap back, it struck him suddenly that he was far better off as Jerry Gordon than as either Schmidt or Little Tom Little.

So let it be.

"Mind what I say!" cried Mrs. Johnson. "Hold him fast. You'll pay, and pay plenty, if he gets away from you!"

"Count on us," said a staker, giving the midget a ferocious shake. "C'mon, Pete."

And between them, the two stakers hauled away Little Tom Little, now Gordon.

Having gotten out of the scrape so neatly, Tommy himself, now bronzed and strong, tall and handsome, felt quite elated about the matter. Plainly he now had his chance. He had the goods on Schmidt. He had merely to turn the tables and wrest the proof, and all was well once more.

He was on the verge of striking a pose and accusing Schmidt of all the crimes he knew the ringmaster guilty of when yet another thing happened.

A long, stirring chord, A major, betokened the introduction of an act in the big top. And Betty snatched at Gordon—Tommy—and cried, "There's your cue!"

And Schmidt echoed it more loudly. "You're holding up the show! They're letting your cats into the arena this instant! Hurry, man, do you want to ruin everything?"

Tommy was engulfed in a terrible thought. Cats—big cats, tawny cats, lions and tigers with gaping fangs and saber claws—waiting for *him*! Waiting to claw and rip, to rend his flesh and destroy him, the way that lion had almost done in St. Louis!

So paralyzed was he that he could not cry out. And neither could he resist Mrs. Johnson and Schmidt, who hurried him swiftly along toward the marquee.

Inside, they were repeating the chord as a conclusion to the announcement, and then once more it wailed forth, anxiously calling for the absent wild animal trainer.

Tommy stopped dragging back. Like a martyr who can already smell the smoke of his fellow victims, he thought it best to put a face upon it and hope that it would not be too slow or painful.

For he might think of standing up to a big person, he might take a chance or two in his act, but never, never could he envision himself facing one big cat, much less forty. Through his mind ran that scene in St. Louis. He could smell again the fetid breath of the brute, could feel once more the rake of butcher-knife claws. If help had come an instant later than it had, it would have been all over.

Looking down at himself as they rushed him along, he could not credit himself with his present body's capabilities. Gordon was strong and handsome and sure. But he was strong and handsome and sure in his soul—and *there* was the difference.

How he had failed! Tommy thought. Bodies did not seem to make any difference at all. It was the soul of the man that counted. What he was deep inside him, what courage and daring he might possess. And if he were the biggest man in the world and possessed no strength of soul, he would still be a fumbling fool.

He had prayed for a chance to prove that it was the body which counted. He had dreamed of being able to prove that, size for size, he could match up with the best of the big world. And now his craven heart, even as he cursed it, told him that he had lied. He was a big person now. No stronger body existed in all this sawdust land than Gordon's. But without the heart and soul of a lion trainer, the body was so much clay, dependent on the Command within it. The man was his soul, not his body.

And Tommy hated himself, realizing that he had not the courage to face those beasts!

In his favor there was the fact that, expert showman though he might be, he had never had any experience whatever with animal training. So deeply had he hated the thought of facing the big cats that he had never even been able to watch Gordon work. And so he couldn't go in and fake a routine, even if he had the nerve. He didn't know one end of that arena from the other. He was Little Tom Little, midget ace, no matter how much the world mistook him for Jerry Gordon, Emperor of the Kings of Beastiana.

With a gasp, he held up again. Somehow he knew that Maizie, standing by the first tier of seats, had been on the outskirts of the last half-hour's events. She had seen and heard all that had passed with Schmidt, for how, otherwise, could poor Maizie know so definitely that she looked at Little Tommy Little now, and not Jerry Gordon?

That she did know was written plainly upon her stricken face. No larger than a child's big doll, prettier even in her grief than many a movie star, she had come to help him. Her intuition had identified him, and now—

Suddenly his heart gave a lurch. Why had she placed herself there? Why, if not to offer him his last chance at life?

And she cried out to him as he passed, "Look at me! Save yourself!"

And she would have reached for him if Schmidt had not hurled her back. Little Tom Little tried to wrench away and strike Schmidt at that. And in doing so, he discovered another truth.

Schmidt understood. He had understood all along! He knew definitely that this was not really Jerry Gordon—knew that a mere midget would curl up and die in that arena under the trampling of clawed feet. Knew that Jerry Gordon would also die in the body . . .

The knowledge was an ice-water bath. Why did he let them carry him on this way? Why didn't he fight?

But Schmidt's grip on his arm was painful. And then—then there were five thousand people under the canvas, watching with bated breath while the trumpets screamed, rolled to announce the approach of Jerry Gordon, Master of Death.

Now a spotlight had them in its grip. He was blinded by it for an instant, and then ahead of him loomed the thin vertical lines which made up the beast arena. He stood all alone, while Mrs. Johnson and Schmidt drew away. While Schmidt leaped up before the band and snatched the speaker mike and bawled:

"Ladees and gennulmun! Pree-senting the one and only mastah of wild beasts in all the cir-cus wurrrld—who dares step into the areena with ta-wenty li-uns and ta-wenty man-eating and ferocious Bengal tigahs, which, though deadly enemies of each othah, though deadly enemies of man, will be fought to complete obedience by one human being, one man who, alone and without help, will step fearlessly into that arena and conquer with a whip and a gun of blanks the absolutely untamable, carnivorous, ravenous, dia-bol-ical, vol-canic, tempestuous, murderous terrors of the jungle. Ladees and gennulmun, I give you the most fearless man who ever trod our earth's fair face, Jerry Gordon, Emperor of the Jungle Monarchs, Master of the Wurrld's most dangerous animals!"

The drums rolled and the trumpets blared.

The spot flashed and crackled and was hot upon him.

Tommy was too much of a showman to run. He was hypnotized by his position. And there was something else. So much was it a habit of this body to step forward and enter that arena, that his traitorous legs were carrying him straight to the side door.

Behind him in the sudden hush he heard just one thin cry. *"Tommy!"*

He would not look back. It would be dangerous. . . .

Out of the run and into the arena spilled the giant cats. Flashing tawny bodies, four and five hundred pounds each brute, every ounce a demander of blood! Stripes and snarls and gleaming teeth all milled just behind these thin grates, racing round and round, swiping at each other, snarling and spitting and roaring death to each other and the menagerie men and the world of people.

Five thousand spectators, with chilled spines, looked upon the scene. Five thousand spectators saw—or thought they saw—Jerry Gordon step into the double doors, shut himself in the separate cage, then poise and steel himself for entrance into the arena itself.

It was death, but he had to go through with it. It was death, but, with these people and the spotlight, he could not go back.

Perhaps he owed that to Gordon. Perhaps this was a last desperate effort to prove himself right, to prove that being a big person in size was quite enough, and that the soul mattered not at all. Perhaps this was his jeer to his own puny courage. He had been terrified of all things—that was why he had wanted to stop being a midget. And though that fear had grown wholly from his minuteness, from the danger of being stepped upon, and the careless way the big world had pushed him around, it was cowardice just the same. Cowardice—and it had driven him to this. And was it not justice, now, that he should face a crucial test?

Maybe—though the hope was faint—maybe he could get away with this. His body had carried him to the right door. It might carry him through the right motions. And these cats were used to Gordon, and now—now wasn't he Gordon?

He had asked for this. He would take it.

The steel bars were cold upon his palm, and he pulled open the second door.

Before him the milling beasts leaped away. A lion sprang to his pedestal, a tiger to his. And then, like an avalanche in reverse, the instant he mechanically cracked his whip and fired his gun, all but one soared upward to their perches. The one backed and clawed at the lash, and spat at the flame and powder smoke. He was a heavy, furious lion, whose mane bristled out to frame his rageful face.

The air was oppressive with the animal smell. The stands

47

were a heaving blur somewhere out beyond the lights. Five thousand faces were less than one.

He, Little Tom Little, was all alone in a wild beast arena, and despite this body which he had usurped, he was still a midget. For, though his hand and arm mechanically cracked that whip and fired the gun, he had forgotten, in his horror, that he was "Jerry Gordon." He might see the size of his arm, he might feel the largeness of his body, but he could not believe these mere manifestations of sense. He was himself, his soul, and that was the soul of Little Tom Little, midget and coward!

With whip and flame, Tommy fought the lion. Sawdust churned beneath his boots. And when the brute reared up and pawed the air, the chair came naturally to his hand. Despite himself, he found that he advanced. To his amazement, the lion pedestaled himself. Tommy could not believe that he had won in this—that the act would run on its usual routine.

But there was a big tiger angrily leaping down to prepare for its hoop act, to be followed by the others in rotation. The tiger went through the hoop, and the whole brutish mass glistened and rippled as beast after beast leaped through the ring.

Little Tom Little began to take heart. For all their snarling and fighting, these animals had been beautifully trained. And they were held in check by the sight and smell of Jerry Gordon, even though Jerry Gordon was not there. . . .

The roll-over tiger came next. So often had that arm given the cue that now it came without Tommy understanding it. Over went the tiger once, but not twice. Here she knew

48

there was a break, a break in which she roared her defiance and advanced, prepared to leap. Gordon, at this point, would advance upon her, chair held against his breast, bending low and glaring hypnotically into her eyes to force her back, to outstare and outface her and, by sheer will, make her lie down and roll once more. And the other beasts knew that they must roar and swap pedestals and glare at their trainer, to make a fighting act.

Up came the chair to Tommy's chest. Forward came the tiger, spitting curses, raking out with lustful claws.

And the routine would have held together, for now Tommy was perceiving that this *was* routine with them all, done so often that neither beasts nor man had to think what came next. They were automatons in a cage, and if he let his body follow through, he would be all right.

But Tommy himself did not know that the roll-over tiger's ferocity was supposed to reach such a hideous pass. For a moment, once more he was fully Little Tom Little. He knew how far behind him he could go—but in his anxiety, he estimated the distance for Little Tom Little, not six-foot-three Jerry Gordon—and took three steps, when he should have taken one.

Just at the point where he was sure he could get through, when he had lost respect for these brutes and the act, his heel caught in an abandoned hoop!

Backwards he went, falling heavily, for it was further down than he had thought. He strove to brace himself up the instant he struck. He wanted to slash with the whip and fire the gun, and then take an instant's rest in the entranceway.

But this act was no fake, nor was it wholly routine. For these were jungle cats, from Malaysia and Africa, and to see their trainer down—

The roll-over tiger sprang. Tommy fired the gun into her open mouth. She screamed and sprang back. But the others had not felt her pain. The others saw only their trainer now—and how many years they had waited for that! How many years had they sat on these pedestals glaring hungrily at this man, biding their time, doing his bidding, waiting for the time when they could smother him with their weight, rake him with their claws, feel his warm flesh between their mighty jaws!

And down they came!

Immediate death was not scheduled by fate in that instant, for a great lion jostled a tiger as they both leaped in the van. Blood enemies, personal enemies, they whirled and met with a thud which shook the bars like straws.

Tommy, in an agony of fear, pitched himself backwards, still striving to gain his feet. He faced about to shout imploringly at the menagerie men. Already spikes were being snatched up and fagots thrust into the cage. But it was slow, slow work, and death was only split instants away.

The warring brutes had touched off the bomb. Released from the constraint of whip and flame, others smashed into each other with all the strength of pent-up hate. Still others remembered the fallen trainer and strove to get at him through the press. The two brutes who had started it, intent upon each other, shifted their warring ground toward Tommy. In a moment they were fighting on top of him, paying him no heed, but blanketing him and trampling him and clawing him just the same.

The tent had gone crazy. Five thousand voices had emitted a single sound, and now again there was silence. The menagerie men poked unavailingly through the bars. Three fought together all at once trying to open the door and drag the trainer out.

"You fools!" screamed a shrill voice. "You fools, get away from that door!"

Tommy, through the haze of battle, saw a sight which came into his consciousness more acutely than even the shock of immediate death.

Somehow Jerry Gordon—the real Jerry Gordon, in the image of Little Tom Little—had fought away from his captors. And now, seeing his beasts tear themselves to bits, seeing his own desired body threatened in war upon the sawdust, about to be slaughtered, he too had forgotten his momentary identity. He belonged in that cage, and he was fighting his way to it.

"Use your gun!" screamed the real Gordon.

And in that instant the thing was again effected. Tommy could not have helped it had he tried. He had been called, the words were hot in his brain, and a moment later all the strain was done. For there he stood, safe outside the cage, staring in at Jerry Gordon, all buried underneath the savage cats!

Here he was safe. He had turned the tables again. There was Gordon in his rightful self. Here was he, Tommy—

Jerry Gordon, beneath the howling hell, blazed away

hysterically with his revolver, straight up into the bodies of
the brutes. But the bite of powder had only one effect. They
had forgotten Gordon. They had been intent upon killing
one another. But the sting in the bellies of the lion and the
tiger made them leap back away from one another and see
their original goal.

Gordon tried to get up, but even he understood that he
would never make it. His whip had vanished. His chair was
a mound of splintered wreckage. And now, as he yanked on
his trigger, his shots only infuriated the animals more, only
drew their attention to him, only started their charge—the
last charge Jerry Gordon would ever see.

The petrified menagerie men had brought up the tear gas,
but so seldom had it been used that the one who threw the
bombs did not pull the catch. Harmlessly they rolled around
on the sawdust, trampled presently out of sight.

The pikes were not long enough, and the wielders showed
no taste for going into that cage through the main door.

Safe outside, Little Tom Little watched. There was
something all wrong about this, something horrible. He
was the cause of Jerry Gordon's coming death. He had done
this to the man—and then he had slipped out of there, to
remain safe and sound outside those bars. Coward! This was
certain proof of it. Craven coward, that's what he was, to
cause another man's death and then let him die!

But a midget thirty inches tall was only a mouthful for any
one of these brutes. He would last no longer than Gordon.
But he had caused it. He had done this thing to an innocent
man.

Stories from the Golden Age

by L. Ron Hubbard

Join the Stories from the Golden Age Book Club Today!

Yes! Sign me up for the Book Club (*check one of the following*) and each month I will receive:

○ One paperback book at $9.95 a month.

○ Or, one unabridged audiobook CD at the cost of $9.95 a month.

Book Club members get FREE SHIPPING and handling (applies to US residents only).

Name _____ (please print)

If under 18, signature of guardian _____

Address _____

City _____ State ____ ZIP ____ Telephone _____

E-mail _____

You may sign up by doing any of the following:

1. To pay by credit card go online at www.goldenagestories.com

2. Call toll-free 1-877-842-5299 or fax this card in to 1-323-466-7817

3. Send in this card with a check for the first month payable to Galaxy Press

To get a FREE Stories from the Golden Age catalog check here ○ and mail or fax in this card.

Thank you!

L. RON HUBBARD

Subscribe today!

And get a FREE gift.

For details, go to www.goldenagestories.com.

BUSINESS REPLY MAIL

FIRST-CLASS MAIL   PERMIT NO. 75738   LOS ANGELES CA

POSTAGE WILL PAID BY ADDRESSEE

GOLDEN AGE BOOK CLUB
GALAXY PRESS
7051 HOLLYWOOD BLVD
LOS ANGELES CA 90028-9771

Jerry Gordon, beneath the howling hell, blazed
away hysterically with his revolver, straight up
into the bodies of the brutes.

It was too much to bear. Safety was nothing compared to these thoughts. With a sharp cry to Gordon, Little Tom Little snatched a torch from an attendant's paralyzed hand and slid through the bars!

He was shaking so in his terror that he could scarcely keep the grip upon the weapon. But he made himself lunge forward like a fencer, straight into the face of the tiger which sprang upon Gordon.

The brute got the torch halfway down its throat. It halted and spun about, and leaped away with a yowl of pain. And the lion on the right transferred his attention to the midget. The lion sprang, got the torch in his chest, and went yelping for the chutes.

Another tiger sprang and another tiger stopped, bowling Tommy over and over, but running out instantly just the same. Battered, Tommy got up. Berserk with rage, he completely forgot his size for the first time in his life. Like a small javelin tipped with flame, he sizzled into the press of fighting cats around Gordon.

They raked at the torch. They screamed. They reared back and fell over themselves to get out of the way. And then they saw their fellows heading for the dark safety of the chute, and, nose to tail, the remainder of the forty plunged out of sight.

The arena was empty of cats. The dust hung in the clash of spotlights. The smoke of the torch wreathed upward to blacken Tommy's face.

Gordon, lying on his side, groaned and turned a little. Then he was still. The bars came down, blocking off the chute.

There was no danger now.

Tommy let the torch fall and stared down at his small hands. He wondered if he were going to be so very ill. It was almost certain that he would be.

There was a clanging and a clatter and the door came open. But it was not an attendant. It was Betty, and her tinsel crown was all in disarray and her fingers were bleeding from tearing so long at the jammed safety lock. She flung herself down beside Jerry, feeling for his heart, trying to cushion his bleeding head.

Men began to swarm into the place. The din out of five thousand throats came like the sound of diving planes.

"Jerry, Jerry!" cried the girl. "Jerry, don't die! You can't die!"

His eyes came open and he stared dazedly at her.

"Jerry!" she whispered brokenly.

He tried to struggle up and got into a sitting position, shaking his head to get the fog out of it.

"Jerry, you were right about Schmidt. I did it . . . only God knows why! You were right, and you'll hate me. But I'll make it up, Jerry. Honest I'll make it up!"

He looked at her for a little while and then took her hand. A doc came, opening his bag, but Jerry Gordon stood up and pushed him back.

"You think these cuts are anything, Doc? Hell, man, I've been sick for weeks and weeks, but this is all I needed!" And, limping, he let Betty help him from the arena.

Mrs. Johnson was struggling to get through the people who surrounded Tommy. He could not hear what men were saying, anyhow. He didn't need what they were saying.

"I . . . I don't know what to say!" said Mrs. Johnson.

"Why say anything?" said Tommy impudently. He fished in his pockets for a handkerchief, but all he could find were letters and small books. Incuriously he hauled them out, and not until they fell from his hand and he had to pick them up did he know what they were.

Suddenly a great light sizzled through him. He flicked open the first bankbook, on which was written "Hermann Schmidt." He stared at the list of deposits, at the tens of thousands of dollars Schmidt had saved in three months out of a salary of a thousand dollars a month. And he stared at a love letter which began "My darling Hermann," and ended "Your Betty."

"But I hardly know—" Mrs. Johnson was saying. "After all, it is a criminal offense to steal—and our profits have been missing. . . ." She dabbed at her eyes. "What . . . what am I going to do?"

"Do?" said Tommy.

And there came Schmidt, all unawed by the scenes which had gone before, having in tow two John Laws, men without imagination or a sense of the fitness of things.

"There he is," said Schmidt, pointing at Tommy. "He almost got away, but—" Then, seeing what Tommy had in his hands, Schmidt, always quick, snatched at them so swiftly that Tommy was forced to let go. "Now take him," said Schmidt. "What he has done just now has no bearing on—"

"Give me that book and that letter!" shrilled Tommy.

Schmidt shoved him off and the two John Laws made a grab at him.

"Give me that book," cried Tommy, "or . . . or I'll tear your heart out!"

Schmidt was on the verge of laughing. But a sharp-toed little boot squarely in the shins turned the laughter into a yelp and a curse. Schmidt grabbed his injured limb and hopped for an instant. Again the John Laws made a snatch. But Tommy wasn't in the space where their hands met.

Tommy wasn't there. He was up on Schmidt's chest like a steeplejack, and he had two thumbs which stabbed into Schmidt's eyes like hot pokers. Schmidt knocked him off.

Tommy lit like a rubber ball, bellowing his battle cry, "Give me that book!" And again he was upon Schmidt.

Perhaps he had learned something from the tigers, or perhaps Schmidt looked small compared to a lion. Anyway, small fists, correctly placed, and small boots stabbing sharp, and a small target which moves faster than the eye can follow will always be superior to slow and heavy brawn. The John Laws gaped in amazement and got in each other's way.

Unwittingly, Schmidt allowed himself to be backed by the attack up to the treacherous hoop which had already done its work. And, stumbling on its low rim, Schmidt tottered and went down. It was no accident that Tommy lit with both feet upon Schmidt's solar plexus.

Schmidt gave an agonized wheeze and tried to fend him off. But Tommy had learned well from the tigers. And though he might weigh but a few pounds and stand but a few inches high, the point to remember was never to give ground.

And Schmidt, the third time the boots landed in his midriff, rolled his eyes whitely back into his head and went out cold.

Now that he was quiet, Tommy was able to retrieve the bankbook and the letter. One John Law had withdrawn so that the other could get their game, but now the other got a bitten hand and felt himself burned from the rear. He whirled and leaped away from the torch in Maizie's hands.

Tommy handed book and letter to Mrs. Johnson. She could not understand immediately and did not really get the idea until Tommy roared, "All right, you two fumbling pachyderms! If you can get *anything* through your thick skulls, *that's* the man you want—Hermann Schmidt!"

Mrs. Johnson looked from book and letter to the recumbent Schmidt, and then, as he was beginning to come around, she booted the red waistcoat once more.

"Get up, you thief! Get up! And as for you two, get that man out of here before I finish what Tommy started. Do you hear?"

Maizie was gazing at Tommy so hungrily that she almost missed the arena door. As he helped her through, she said in a choked voice, "I knew when you were *you*, Tommy. I *knew*. And when you jumped in through the bars—"

"Forget it," said Tommy with a grin. "You were right and I was wrong. But I was right, too, you see, because . . . because . . . well, if the ghost of the Professor is around, I'll bet he's plenty disappointed. He did me a favor, Maizie. He showed me that I was a selfish fool, a coward. I'm ashamed of myself. I didn't think of you at all when I started this. I won't ever do it again, Maizie. Never . . . I promise!"

Maizie's eyes were very bright.

"And you'll come back and be satisfied to be—a freak?"

"No!" cried Tommy. "Who said anything about going back? Look up there, Maizie!"

She saw that they stood under the mike platform. She felt a movement at her side and, startled, saw Tommy run up the steps. She saw him tip over the mike so that he could get it down to his height and then, brazenly from the speakers, she heard his best spieling voice.

"Ladees an' gennulmen! Whatevah may happen in a circus, the show must go on! And it gives me pleasure to present to you, for your entertainment, an attraction which we have brought to you at great expense."

It was Tommy the Showman, Tommy at his best, doing what he had longed to do, realizing the ambition that had burned all these years in his frail but valiant little body.

Tommy was glowing, vivid, terrifically alive—and happier than he had ever been in all his life.

Maizie's breath caught in her throat. Suppose that happiness should be taken from him! Suppose he lost it now, in the moment that fulfilled his long-cherished dream! It would break his heart if—

Bewildered by the turn of events, Maizie looked from Tommy to Mrs. Johnson, across the hoople. But Mrs. Johnson was looking at five thousand spectators whose attention was riveted upon a minute figure by the mike, a figure whose voice even more than his bravery, whose handsomeness even more than his smallness, commanded their every faculty!

And Mrs. Johnson, gazing back at Little Tom Little, had a look upon her face which clearly wondered why nobody had ever thought of this before. She saw Maizie, then, with questioning eyes upon her. And to Maizie Mrs. Johnson smiled and very slowly nodded her much wiser old head. . . .

THE LAST DROP

THE LAST DROP

EUCLID O'BRIEN'S assistant, Harry McLeod, looked at the bottle on the bar with the air of a man who has just received a dare.

Mac was no ordinary bartender—at least in his own eyes if not in those of the saloon's customers—and it had been his private dream for years to invent a cocktail which would burn itself upon the pages of history. So far his concoctions only burned gastronomically.

Euclid had dismissed the importance of this bottle as a native curiosity, for it had been sent from Borneo by Euclid's brother, Aristotle. Perhaps Euclid had dismissed the bottle because it made him think of how badly he himself wanted to go to Borneo.

Mac, however, had not dismissed it. Surreptitiously Mac pulled the cork and sniffed. Then, with determination, he began to throw together random ingredients—whiskey, yolk of an egg, lemon and a pony of this syrup Euclid's brother had sent.

Mac shook it up.

Mac drank it down.

"Hey," said Euclid belatedly. "Watcha doin'?"

"Mmmmm," said Mac, eyeing the three customers and Euclid, "that is what I call a *real* cocktail! Whiskey, egg yolk, lemon, one pony of syrup. Here"—he began to throw together another one—"try it!"

"No!" chorused the customers.

Mac looked hurt.

"Gosh, you took an awful chance," said Euclid. "I never know what Aristotle will dig up next. He said to go easy on that syrup because the natives said it did funny things. He says the native name, translated, means *swello*."

"It's swell all right," said Mac. Guckenheimer, one of the customers, looked at him glumly.

"Well," snapped Mac, "I ain't dead yet."

Guckenheimer continued to look at him. Mac looked at the quartet.

"Hell, even if I do die, I ain't giving you the satisfaction of a free show." And he grabbed his hat and walked out.

Euclid looked after him. "I hope he don't get sick."

Guckenheimer looked at the cocktail Mac had made and shook his head in distrust.

Suddenly Guckenheimer gaped, gasped and then wildly gesticulated. "Look! Oh, my God, look!"

A fly had lighted upon the rim of the glass and had imbibed. And now, before their eyes, the fly expanded, doubled in size, trebled, quadrupled . . .

Euclid stared in horror at this monster, now the size of a small dog, which feebly fluttered and flopped about on shaking legs. It was getting bigger!

Euclid threw a bung starter with sure aim. Guckenheimer and the other two customers beat it down with chairs. A few seconds later they began to breathe once more.

Euclid started to drag the fly toward the garbage can and then stopped in horror. "M-Mac drank some of that stuff!"

Guckenheimer sighed. "Probably dead by now then."

"But we can't let him wander around like that! Swelling up all over town! Call the cops! Call somebody! Find him!"

Guckenheimer went to the phone, and Euclid halted in rapid concentration before his tools of trade.

"I gotta do something. I gotta do something," he gibbered.

Chivvis, a learned customer, said, "If that stuff made Mac swell up, it might make him shrink too. If he used lemon for his, he got an acid reaction. Maybe if you used limewater for yours, you would get an alkaline reaction."

Euclid's paunch shook with his activity. Larkin, the third customer, caught a fly and applied it to the swello cocktail. The fly rapidly began to get very big. Euclid picked up the loathsome object and dunked its proboscis in some of his limewater cocktail. Like a plane fading into the distance, it grew small.

"It works!" cried Euclid. "Any sign of Mac?"

"Nobody has seen anything yet," said Guckenheimer. "If anything does happen to him and he dies, the cops will probably want you for murder, Euclid."

"Murder? Me? Oh! I shoulda left this business years ago. I shoulda got out of New York while the going was good. I shoulda done what I always wanted and gone to Borneo! Guckenheimer, you don't think they'll pin it on me if anything happens to Mac?"

Guckenheimer suddenly decided not to say anything. Chivvis and Larkin, likewise, stopped talking to each other.

A man had entered the bar—a man who wore a Panama hat and a shoulder-padded suit of the latest Broadway design, a man who had a narrow, evil face.

Frankie Guanella sat down at the bar and beckoned commandingly to Euclid.

"Okay, O'Brien," said Guanella, "this is the first of the month."

O'Brien had longed for Borneo for more reasons than one, but that one was big enough—Frankie Guanella, absolute monarch of the local corner gang, who exacted his tribute with regularity.

"I ain't got any dough," said O'Brien, made truculent by Mac's possible trouble.

"No?" said Guanella. "O'Brien, we been very reasonable. The las' guy who wouldn't pay out a policy got awful boint when his jernt boined down."

And just to show his aplomb, Guanella reached out and tossed off one of the cocktails which had been used on the flies.

In paralyzed horror the four stared at Guanella, wondering if he would go up or shrink.

"Hey, who's the funny guy?" said Guanella, snatching off his hat, his voice getting shriller. He looked at the band. "No, it's got my 'nitials." He clapped it back on and it fell over his face.

With a squeal of alarm he tumbled off the stool. Whatever he intended to do, he was floundering around the floor in clothes twice too big for him. Shrill, mouselike squeaks issued from the pile of clothing. Chivvis and Larkin and Guckenheimer looked around bug-eyed. Presently the Panama detached itself from the pile of clothes and began to run around the room on a pair of small bare legs.

A customer had just come in, and had started to climb a stool. He looked long and carefully at the hat. Then he began tiptoeing out. Before he reached the door, the hat started toward the door also. The customer went out with an audible swish, the hat scuttling after him.

"Oh, my!" said O'Brien. "He won't like that. No, sir! He's sensitive about his size anyway. We better do something before he brings his whole mob back. Will you telephone again, Mr. Guckenheimer?"

As Guckenheimer moved to do so, O'Brien went into furious action to make another shrinko cocktail. He was just about to add the syrup when the shaker skidded out of his trembling hands and smashed on the floor. O'Brien took a few seconds of hard breathing to get himself under control. Then he hunted up another shaker and began over again. If Mac's swello cocktail had contained a pony of syrup, an equal amount in the shrinko cocktail ought to just reverse the effect. He made a triple quantity just to be on the safe side.

Guckenheimer waddled back from the booth.

"They found him!" he cried. "He's down by the McGraw-Hill building, hanging on to the side. He says he doesn't dare let go for fear his legs will break under his weight!"

"That's right," said Chivvis. "It accords with the square-cube law. The cross-sectional area, and hence the strength in compression, of his leg bones would not increase in proportion to his mass—"

"Oh, forget it, Chivvis!" snapped Larkin. "If we don't hurry—"

"—he'll be dead before we can help him," finished Guckenheimer.

O'Brien was hunting for a thermos bottle he remembered having seen. He found it, and had just poured the shrinko cocktail into it and screwed the cap on when three men entered the Hole in the Wall. One of them carried Frankie Guanella in the crook of his arm. Guanella, now a foot tall, had a handkerchief tied diaperwise around himself. The three diners, now the only customers in the place, started to rise.

One of the newcomers pointed a pistol at them, and said conversationally, "Sit down, gents. And keep your hands on the table. Thass right."

"Whatchgonnado?" said O'Brien, going pale under his ruddiness.

"Don't get excited, Jack. You got an office in back, ain'tcha? We'll use it for the fight."

"Fight?"

"Yep. Frankie says nothing will satisfy him but a dool. He's sensitive about his size, poor little guy."

"But—"

"I know. You're gonna say it wouldn't be fair, you being so much bigger'n him. But we'll fix that. You make some more of that poison you gave him, so you'll both be the same size."

"But I haven't any more of the stuff!"

"Too bad, Jack. Then I guess we'll just have to let you have it. We was going to give you a sporting chance, too." And he raised the gun.

"No!" cried O'Brien. "You can't—"

"What's he got in that thermos bottle?" piped Frankie.

"Make him show it. He just poured it outa that glass and it smells the same!"

"Don't!" yelped O'Brien. He grabbed at the bottle of Borneo syrup and the thermos in the vain hope of beating his way out. But too many hands were reaching for him.

And then came catastrophe! The zealous henchmen, in their tackle, sent both syrup and thermos flying against the beer taps. The splinter of glass was music in O'Brien's ears. The syrup was splattered beyond retrieve, for most of it had gone down the drain. But O'Brien had no more than started to breathe when he realized that only the syrup bottle had broken. The thermos, no matter how jammed up inside, still contained the shrinko cocktail.

What would happen now? If he drank that shrinko he might never, never, never again be able to get any syrup to swell up again!

One of the gangsters, having vaulted the bar, was unscrewing the thermos for Frankie's inspection. Smelling of it, Frankie announced that it was the right stuff, all right, all right. Another gangster came over the bar.

And then O'Brien was upon his back on the duckboards and a dose of shrinko was being forcibly administered. He gagged and choked and swore, but it went on down just the same.

"There," said one of the men in a satisfied voice. "Now shrink, damn you."

He put the cap back on the bottle and the bottle on the bar, mentally listing a number of persons who might benefit from a dose.

The first thing O'Brien noticed was the looseness of his clothes. He instinctively reached for his belt to tighten it, but he knew it would do no permanent good.

"Come on in the office, all of you," said the gangster lieutenant. He prodded the three customers and O'Brien ahead of him. O'Brien tripped over his drooping pants. As he reached the office door he fell sprawling. A gangster booted him and he slid across the floor, leaving most of his clothes behind him. The remaining garments fell off when he struggled to his feet. The walls and ceiling were receding. The men and the furniture were both receding and growing to terrifying size.

He was shivering with cold, though the late-May air was warm. And he felt marvelously light. He jumped up, feeling as active as a terrier despite his paunch. He was sure he could jump to twice his own height.

"Watch the door, Vic," said the head gangster. His voice sounded to O'Brien like a cavernous rumble. One of his companions opened the door a little and stood with his face near the crack. The head gangster put down Guanella, who was now O'Brien's own size. Guanella had a weapon that looked to O'Brien like an enormous battle-ax, until he realized that it consisted of an unshaped pencil split lengthwise, with a razor blade inserted in the cleft, and the whole tied fast with string. Guanella swung his ponderous-looking weapon as if it were a feather.

The head gangster said, "Frankie couldn't pull a trigger no more, so he figured this out all by himself. He's smott."

Guanella advanced across the floor toward O'Brien. He was smiling, and there was death in his sparkling black eyes. No weapon had been produced for O'Brien, but then he did not really expect one. This was a gangster's idea of a sporting chance.

Guanella leaped forward and swung. The razor-ax went *swish,* but O'Brien had jumped back just before it arrived. His agility surprised both himself and Guanella, who had never fought under these grasshoppery conditions. Guanella rushed again with an overhead swing. O'Brien jumped to one side like a large pink cricket. Guanella swung across. O'Brien, with a mighty leap, sailed clear over Guanella's head. He fell when he landed, but bounced to his feet without appreciable effort.

Around they went. O'Brien, despite his chill, did not feel at all tired, though a corresponding amount of exercise would have laid him up if he had been his normal size. The laughter of the men thundered through the room. O'Brien thought unhappily that as soon as they became bored with this spectacle they would tie a weight to him to make him easier game for their man.

Then a reflection caught his eye. It was a silvery spike lying in a crack of the floor. He snatched it up. It was an ordinary pin, not at all sharp, to his vision, but it would do for a dagger.

Guanella approached, balancing his ax. The minute he raised it, O'Brien leaped at him, stabbing. The point bounced back from Guanella's hide, which seemed much tougher than ordinary human skin had a right to be. Down they went.

The razor-ax went swish, *but O'Brien had jumped back just before it arrived. His agility surprised both himself and Guanella, who had never fought under these grasshoppery conditions.*

Their mutual efforts buffeted O'Brien about so that he hardly knew what he was doing. But he got a glimpse of Guanella's arm flat on the floor, the handle—the eraser end—of the ax gripped in his fist. With both hands O'Brien drove the point of his pin into the arm. It went in and through and into the wood. Guanella shouted. O'Brien caught up the ax and raced for the door.

He moved so quickly, compared to his normal ponderousness, that the gangsters were caught flat-footed. O'Brien slashed with the rear edge at the ankle of the man at the door. He saw the sock peel down, and the oozing skin after it. Vic roared and jumped, almost stepping on O'Brien, who dashed through and out.

He raced to the bar; a mighty jump took him to the top of a stool, and thence he jumped to the bar-top. He gathered the thermos bottle under his arm. It was a small thermos bottle, but it was still almost as big as he was. But he had no time to ponder on the wonders of size. There was a thunderous explosion behind him, and a bullet ripped along the bar, throwing splinters large enough to bowl him over. He hopped off onto a stool, and thence to the floor, and raced out. He zigzagged, and the shots that followed him went wide.

Outside, he yelled, "Orson!"

Orson Crow, O'Brien's favorite hackman, looked up from his tabloid. Seeing O'Brien bearing down on him, he muttered something about seeing things, and trod on the starter.

"Wait!" shouted O'Brien. "It's me, Obie! Let me in, quick! Quick, I say!"

He pounded on the door of the cab. Crow still did not recognize him, but at that minute a gangster with a pistol appeared at the door of the Hole in the Wall. Crow at least understood that this animated billiken was being pursued with felonious intent. So he threw open the door, almost knocking O'Brien over. O'Brien leaped in.

"McGraw-Hill building, quick!" he gasped. Crow automatically started to obey the order. As the cab roared down Eighth Avenue, O'Brien explained what he could to the bewildered driver.

"Well, now," he said, "have you got a handkerchief?" When Crow produced one, not exactly clean, O'Brien tied it diaperwise around his middle.

When they reached the McGraw-Hill building, they did not have to ask where McLeod was. There was a huge crowd, and many firemen and policemen in evidence. Some men were trying to rig up a derrick. A searchlight on a firetruck played on the unfortunate McLeod, whose fingers clutched the twenty-first story of the building, and whose feet rested on the pavement. He had had difficulty in the matter of clothes similar to that experienced by O'Brien and Guanella, except that he had, of course, grown out of his clothes instead of shrinking out from under them. Around his waist was wound several turns of rope, and through this in front was thrust an uprooted tree, roots up.

A cop stopped the cab. "You can't go no closer."

"But—" said Crow.

"Gawan, I says you can't go no closer."

O'Brien said, "Meet me on the south side of the building, Orson. And open this damn door first."

Crow opened the door. O'Brien scuttled out with his thermos bottle. He scurried through the darkness. The first cop did not even see him. The other persons who saw him did not have a chance to investigate, and assumed that they had suffered a brief illusion. In a few minutes he had dodged around the crowd to the front doors of the building. A fireman saw him coming, but watched him, popeyed, without trying to stop him as he raced through the front door. He kept on through the green-walled corridors until he found a stairway, and started up.

After one flight, he regretted this attempt. The treads were waist-high, and he was getting too tired to leap them, especially with his arms full of thermos bottle. He bounced around to the elevators. The night elevators were working, but the button was far above his reach.

He sat down, panting, for a while. Then he got up and wearily climbed down the whole flight of steps again. He found the night elevator on the ground floor, with the door open.

There was nothing to do but walk in, for all the risks of delay and exposure to Guanella's friends that such a course involved. The operator did not notice his entrance, and when he spoke the man jumped a foot.

"Say," he said, "could you take me up to the floor where the giant's head is?"

The operator looked wildly around the cab. When he saw O'Brien he recoiled as from an angry rattlesnake.

"Well, now," said O'Brien, "you don't have to be scared of me. I just want to go up to give the big guy his medicine."

"You can go up, or you can go back to hell where you came from," said the operator. "I'm off the stuff for life, I swear!" and then he bolted.

O'Brien wondered what to do now. Then he looked over the controls. He swarmed up onto the operator's stool, and found that he could just reach the button marked "18" with his thermos bottle. He thumped the button and pulled down on the starter handle. The elevator started up with a rush.

When it stopped, he went out and wandered around the half-lit corridors looking for the side to which McLeod clung. He was completely turned around by now. But his attention was drawn by a rushing, roaring, pulsating sound coming from one corridor. He trotted down that way.

It was all very well to be able to move more actively than you could ordinarily, but O'Brien was beginning to get tired of the enormous distances he had to cover. And the thermos bottle was beginning to weigh tons.

Euclid O'Brien soon found what was causing the racket. It was the tornado of breath going in and out of McLeod's nose, a part of which could be seen directly in front of the window at the end of the corridor. The nose was a really alarming spectacle. It was lit up with a crisscross of lights from the street lamps and searchlights outside, and by the corridor lights inside. The pores were big enough for O'Brien to stick his thumb into. Sweat ran down it in rippling sheets.

He took a deep breath and jumped from the floor to the

windowsill. He could not possibly open the window. But he took a tight grip on the thermos bottle and banged it against the glass. The glass broke.

O'Brien set the thermos bottle down on the sill, put his hands to his mouth, and yelled, "Hey, Mac!"

Nothing happened. Then O'Brien thought about his voice. He remembered that Guanella's had gone up in pitch when Guanella had drunk the shrinko. No doubt his, O'Brien's, voice had done likewise. But his voice sounded normal to him, whereas those of ordinary-sized men sounded much deeper. So it followed that something had happened to his hearing as well. Which, for O'Brien, was pretty good thinking.

It was reasonable to infer that both McLeod's voice and McLeod's hearing had gone down in pitch when McLeod had gone up in stature. So that to McLeod, O'Brien's voice would be a batlike squeak, if indeed he could hear it at all.

O'Brien lowered his voice as much as he could and bellowed, in his equivalent of a deep bass, "Hey, Mac! It's Obie!"

At last the nose moved, and a huge watery eye swam into O'Brien's vision.

"Ghwhunhts?" said McLeod. At least it sounded like that to O'Brien—a deep rumbling, like that of an approaching subway train.

"Raise your voice!" shouted O'Brien. "Talk—you know—falsetto!"

"Like this?" replied McLeod. His voice was still a deep groan, but it was at least high enough to be intelligible to O'Brien, who clung to the broken edge of the glass while the blast of steamy air from McLeod's lungs tore past him, whipping his diaper.

"Yeah! It's Obie!"

"Who'd you say? Can't recognize you."

"Euclid O'Brien! I got some stuff to shrink you back with!"

"Oh, Obie! You don't look no bigger'n a fly! Did you get shrunk, or have I growed some more?"

"Frankie Guanella's mob shrunk me."

"Well, for heaven's sake do something for me! I can't get my breath, and I'm gonna pass out with the heat, and my legs are gonna bust any minute! I can't hold on to this building much longer!"

O'Brien waved the thermos bottle.

McLeod thundered: "Whazzat, a pill?"

"It's a shrinko cocktail! It'll work all right, on account of that's what shrunk me. If I can get it open . . ." O'Brien was wrestling with the screw cap. "Here! Can you take this cap between your fingernails and hold on while I twist?"

Carefully McLeod released the grip of one of his hands on the windowsills. He groaned at the increased strain on his legs, but the overloaded bones held somehow. He put his free hand up to O'Brien's window. O'Brien carefully inserted the cap between the nails of the thumb and forefinger.

"Now pinch, slowly," he cried. "Not too tight. That's enough!" He turned the flask while McLeod held the cap.

"All right now, Mac, drop the cap and take hold of the cork!" McLeod did so. O'Brien maneuvered the thermos so that its neck was braced in an angle of the hole in the glass. "Now pull, slow!" he called. The cork came out. O'Brien

78

almost fell backwards off the sill. He clutched at the edge of the glass. It would have cut his hand if he had been larger.

"Stick your mouth up here!"

O'Brien never realized what a repulsive thing a human mouth can be until McLeod's vast red lips came moistly pouting up at him.

"Closer!" he yelled. He poured the cocktail into the cavern. "Okay, you'll begin to shrink in a few seconds—I hope."

Presently he observed that McLeod's face was actually a little lower.

"You're shrinking!" he shouted.

The horrible mouth grinned up at him. "You got me just in time!" it roared. "I'd 'a been a dead bartender in another minute."

"There he is!" shouted somebody behind O'Brien in the corridor. O'Brien looked around. Down toward him ran the three unshrunken gangsters.

He yelled to McLeod, "Mac! Put me on your shoulder, quick!"

McLeod reached for him. O'Brien scrambled out on the window ledge and jumped onto the outstretched palm, which transferred him to McLeod's bare shoulder. He observed that McLeod's fingers were bruised and bloody from the strain they had taken in contact with the windowsills. He found a small hair and clung to this. The gangsters' faces appeared at the window a few feet above him. One of them pointed a gun out through the hole in the pane. McLeod made a snatch at the window with his free hand. The faces disappeared like magic, and O'Brien, over the roar of McLeod's breath and the clamor in the street far below, fancied he heard the clatter of fleeing feet in the building.

"What happened?" asked McLeod, turning his head slightly and rolling his eyes in an effort to focus on the mite on his shoulder.

O'Brien explained, as the windows drifted up past him, shouting up into McLeod's ear. As they came nearer the street, O'Brien saw hats blown off by the hurricane of McLeod's breathing. He also saw an ambulance on the edge of the crowd. He figured the ambulance guys must have felt pretty damn silly when they saw the size of their patient.

"What you gonna do next?" asked McLeod. "Swell yourself up? I'd like to help you against Frankie's gang, but I gotta go to the hospital. My arches are ruined if there isn't anything else wrong with me."

"No," said O'Brien. "I got a better idea. Yes, sir. You just put me down when you get small enough to let go the building."

Story by story, McLeod lowered himself as he shrank. Soon he was a mere twenty feet tall.

He said, "I can put you down now, Obie."

"Okay," said O'Brien. At McLeod's sudden stooping movement, the nearest people started back. McLeod was still something pretty alarming to have around the house. O'Brien started running again. And again his small size and the uncertain light enabled him to dodge through the crowd before anybody could stop him. He tore around the corner, and then around another corner, and came to Orson Crow's cab. He banged on the door and hopped in.

"Frankie's mob is after me!" he gasped.

"Where you wanna go, Chief?" asked Crow, who was now fazed by few things.

"Where could a guy a foot tall buy a suit of clothes this time of night? I'm cold."

Crow thought for a few seconds. "Some of the big drugstores carry dolls," he said doubtfully.

"Well, now, you go round to the biggest one you can find, Orson."

They drew up in front of a drugstore.

O'Brien said, "Now, you go in and buy me one of these dolls. And phone one of the papers to find out what pier a boat for the Far East sails from."

"What about the dough, Obie? You owe me a buck on the meter already."

"You collect from Mac. Tell him I'll send it to him as soon as I get to Borneo. Yeah, and get me a banana from that stand. I'm starving."

Crow went. O'Brien squirmed around on the seat, trying not to show himself to passing pedestrians and at the same time keeping an apprehensive eye out for Frankie's friends.

Crow got back in and started the motor as a huge and slightly battered-looking sedan drew up. O'Brien slid to the floor, but not quickly enough. The crack of a pistol was followed by the tinkle of glass as the cab started with a furious rush.

O'Brien, on the floor, was putting on the doll's clothes. "Where's that boat leaving from?"

"Pier eleven, on South Street."

"Make it snappy, Orson."

"What does it look like I'm doing? Taking a sun bath?"

When they reached the pier, there was no sign of the gangsters. O'Brien tumbled out with his banana.

He said, "Better scram, Orson. They'll be along. Yes, sir."

"I'll see that you get off foist," said Crow. O'Brien scuttled down the pier to where the little freighter lay. Her screws had just begun to turn, and seamen were casting loose the hawsers. Crow glimpsed a small mite, barely visible in the darkness, running up a bow rope. It vanished—at least he thought it did—but just then the gangsters' car squealed to a stop beside him. They had seen, too. They piled out and ran down to the ship. The gangplank was up, and the ship was sliding rapidly out of her berth, stern first.

One of the gangsters yelled, "Hey!" at the ship, but nobody paid any attention.

A foot-high, Frankie Guanella capered on the pier in front of the gangsters in excess of homicidal rage. He shrieked abuse at the dwindling ship. When he ran out of words for a moment, Crow, who was climbing back into his cab to make a quiet getaway, heard a faint, shrill voice raised in a tinny song from the shadows around the bow hatches.

It sang, "On the road to Mandalay-ay, where the flying fishes play-ay-ay!"

Crow was too far away to see. But Frankie Guanella saw. He saw the reduced but still-round figure of Euclid O'Brien standing on top of a hatch, holding aloft his bloody ax in one hand. Then the figure vanished into the shadows again.

Guanella gave a choked squeak, and foamed at the mouth.

Before his pals could stop him, he bounded to the edge of the pier and dove off. He appeared on the surface, swimming strongly toward the SS *Leeuwarden*, bobbing blackly in the path of moonlight on the dirty water.

Then a triangular fin—not over a couple of inches high, but still revealing its kinship to its relatives, the sharks—cut the water. The dogfish swirled past Frankie, and there was no more midget swimmer. There was only the moonlight, and the black hull of the freighter swinging around to start on her way to Hong Kong and Singapore.

STORY PREVIEW

Story Preview

NOW that you've just ventured through some of the captivating tales in the Stories from the Golden Age collection by L. Ron Hubbard, turn the page and enjoy a preview of *Danger in the Dark*. Join Billy Newman, who has newly purchased a South Seas island only to discover it's haunted by the giant shark-god Tadamona. Unfortunately the sharp-toothed entity wants more than ritual sacrifice; it's bent on destroying the entire island unless Billy battles it out like David (without the slingshot) versus Goliath!

DANGER IN THE DARK

THE medicine drums were beating wearily and another, greater drum had commenced to boom with a hysteria which spoke of breaking nerves. The slither and slap of bare feet sounded upon Billy's verandah, and he straightened up to see that Wanoa and several lesser chiefs had come.

They greeted him with deep bows, their faces stiff to hide the terror within them.

"Hafa?" said Billy, giving it the "What's the matter" intonation.

"We come to seek your help," said Wanoa.

"I have done all I can," replied Billy. "But if you think what little medicine I have may stave off any new case . . ." He got slowly to his feet and reached mechanically for his topee, although it was already night.

"Medicine does no good," said Wanoa with dignity. "We have found it necessary to use strong means—" He paused, cutting the flow of his Chamorro off short, as though he realized that what he was about to say would not go well with the mahstah.

"And?" said Billy, feeling it somehow.

"We turn back to old rite. Tonight we sacrifice young girl to Tadamona. Maybe it will be that he will turn away his anger—"

"A young girl?" gaped Billy. "You mean . . . you're going to kill—"

"We are sorry. It is necessary. Long time ago priests come. They tell us about fellah mahstah Jesus Christ. We say fine. Bime-by island got nothing but crosses. Tadamona is boss god Kaisan. Tadamona does not like to be forgotten. For a long time he slept. And then he see no sacrifices coming anymore. He get angry. For thirty years we get no rest. We get sick, all the best people die, the crops are bad, the typhoons throw our houses down. Then white men here get plenty power and Tadamona jealous and not like. Things get worse and worse. Tadamona no like white man because white man say he is boss. Tadamona is boss."

"You can't do this," said Billy quietly. "I won't let you murder—"

"We not murder anybody," said Wanoa. "Christina say she happy to die if people get saved."

"Christina! Why, she . . . she's a mission girl! You're lying! She's half-white! She would never consent to such a thing!"

Wanoa made a beckoning motion at the door, and Christina came shyly inside to stand with downcast face.

Billy walked toward her and placed his hand on her shoulder. Very often these last months he had watched her and wondered why he should go on forever alone. He would spend the rest of his life here, and Christina—she had that fragile beauty of the mestiza, beauty enough to turn the heads of most white men.

"You consented to this?" said Billy.

She nodded, not looking at him.

"Christina, you know something of white ways. You know what you have been taught. This Tadamona—why, he is nothing but airy mist. He is a superstition born out of typhoons and sickness and the minds of men who know little. Tadamona does not exist except in your imagination, and your death could do nothing to drive off this plague. You would only add another gravestone in the cemetery, and all the village would weep for you when the disease went on unabated." And as she did not seem to be listening, he raised his voice with sudden fury. "You fools! Your island god doesn't live! He never did live, and he never will! Give me this week and I'll stop this plague! Obey my orders and it will take no more of your people! Tadamona! Damn such a rotten idea!"

They stared at him with shocked attitudes, then glanced uneasily out into the darkness.

"You must not speak so," said Christina in a hushed voice. "He . . . he will come for you."

"How can he come for me if he doesn't exist?" cried Billy.

"You have seen the footprints in the rock," said Wanoa.

"A trick of lava!" shouted Billy. "No man or god has feet ten feet long!"

"You have heard him grumbling in the caverns of the point," said Wanoa.

"A trick of the sea in hollow coral!"

"You have seen where he has torn up palms by the roots," persisted Wanoa.

"They were ready to fall at the slightest breeze. I tell you,

you can't do this! Tadamona is in your heads, and only in your heads, do you understand? If he lives, why haven't I seen him? Why?"

"He is too cunning for that," said Wanoa. "And to see him, to look him full in the face, is to die. Those of our people who have seen him have been found dead, unmarked, in the streets. The wise ones here never stir about after midnight."

"Bah! If he exists let him come and show himself to me! Let him walk up that path and call on me!"

They shrank back away from him as though expecting him to fall dead on the instant. Even Christina moved until his hand fell from her arm.

He was tired again. He felt so very alone and so small. "You can't do this, Christina. Give me a week and I'll stop this plague. I promise it. If I do not, then do what you like. But give me that."

"More people will die," said Christina. "I am not afraid."

"It is the white blood in her," said Wanoa. "It will quiet Tadamona. In a week, we will lose many, many more."

Billy walked up and down the grass mat for minutes. He was weary unto death himself, and these insistent voices bored like awls into his skull. Again he flared:

"So a week is too much to give me?"

"You have had a week," said Wanoa impassively.

Billy faced them, his small face flushed under the flickering hurricane lantern, the wind from the sea stirring his silky blond hair. For the moment he filled his narrow jacket completely. "Yes, damn you, I've had a week! A week obstructed by your yap-yap-yap about Tadamona. If a week is too much, how many days?"

"One day," said Wanoa. "Not many people die in one day."

"One day?" cried Billy. "What— All right," he said, jacket emptying again. "One day. And when that is through I suppose . . ." He glanced at Christina and saw that she would hold to her word then.

To find out more about *Danger in the Dark* and how you can obtain your copy, go to www.goldenagestories.com.

GLOSSARY

GLOSSARY

STORIES FROM THE GOLDEN AGE *reflect the words and expressions used in the 1930s and 1940s, adding unique flavor and authenticity to the tales. While a character's speech may often reflect regional origins, it also can convey attitudes common in the day. So that readers can better grasp such cultural and historical terms, uncommon words or expressions of the era, the following glossary has been provided.*

---

bale ring: in a large tent, the canvas is perforated by holes where the support poles will be. Each hole is fitted with a sturdy metal ring, which is a bale ring. The poles are placed in the rings as the canvas lies on the ground and the rings are raised up the poles by ropes using block and tackle.

bale ring to stakes: everything and everybody; the whole circus.

billiken: a doll created in 1908 that had elf-like pointed ears, a mischievous smile and a tuft of hair on its pointed head. It was a symbol of good luck. Named after its manufacturer, the Billiken Company of Chicago.

bime-by: by and by; eventually.

Black Forest: a wooded mountain range in southwestern Germany. It is known for its highlands, scenery and woods, and in early times it was impenetrable. The Black Forest region is blessed with a particularly rich mythological landscape. It is said to be haunted by werewolves, sorcerers, witches, the devil in differing guises and helpful dwarves who try to balance the scales.

Borneo: the third largest island in the world, located in southeastern Asia.

Brobdingnagian: of or relating to a gigantic person or thing; comes from the book *Gulliver's Travels* of 1726 by Jonathan Swift, wherein Gulliver meets the huge inhabitants of Brobdingnag. It is now used in reference to anything huge.

bull man: bull hand or bull handler; circus employee who works with the elephants.

bung starter: a wooden mallet used for tapping on the bung (cork or stopper) to loosen it from a barrel.

Chamorro: a people inhabiting the Mariana Islands; also the language of these people.

chumps: suckers; people who are gullible and easy to take advantage of.

coconuts, string of: money, especially a large number of bills.

Colossus of Rhodes: a giant statue of the Greek sun god Helios, known by the Romans as the god Apollo. Considered one of the Seven Wonders of the World, the statue stood at the entrance to the harbor of Rhodes, a Greek island, for approximately fifty-five years. It was built in 280 BC to commemorate the island's survival of a year-long siege. Made of bronze and stone with reinforcements of iron inside, the Colossus measured about 120 feet in height. It is sometimes said to have straddled the harbor so that ships sailing in and out went under its legs and is depicted in one account as shielding its eyes from the sun with one hand.

crumb castle: cookhouse; where the circus crew eat.

de facto: exercising power or serving a function without being legally or officially established.

dogfish: a small bottom-dwelling shark with a long tail.

fagots: bundles of sticks, twigs or branches bound together and used as fuel, a torch, etc.

G-men: government men; agents of the Federal Bureau of Investigation.

governor: the head of the show.

gravedigger: a hyena.

hackman: the driver of a hack or taxi.

hawsers: cables or ropes used in mooring or towing ships.

high traps: trapezes high in the air or the people who work them.

high wire: a tightwire act high in the air, or the performer on it.

hoople: ring; the circle in which circus acts are presented. The center ring is about forty-two feet in diameter. It is heavily made, as it is where most of the animal acts perform, and it has to be strong enough for the horses to walk on.

horse piano: calliope; a musical instrument consisting of a series of steam whistles played like an organ. Mounted on a horse-drawn wagon, it is part of the circus parade. It is typically very loud and produces sound that can travel for miles.

howdy: howdah; a seat on the back of an elephant or camel.

John Law: an officer of the law.

Juggernaut car: a large forty-five-foot-tall, multi-ton chariot used in India during annual Hindu processions in honor of Krishna, also called *Jagannatha* (meaning "Lord of the Universe"). Devotees have sometimes been crushed accidentally as the massive car slipped out of control. Many have also been killed in the resulting stampedes. The sight has led to the use of the word *juggernaut* to refer to other instances of unstoppable, crushing forces.

juice joint: a midway concession stand; refreshment stand.

kick 'em: kickoff parade; the making of a street parade to bring people in to see the circus. Developed in the mid-nineteenth century, the circus paraded through the streets to announce its arrival and to drum up business in the community. Such parades featured marching elephants, caged lions and tigers in circus wagons, clowns, etc.

kife: the act of bilking the locals of their money; swindle.

kinker: acrobat or contortionist.

lot lice: local townspeople who arrive early to watch the unloading of the circus and stay late.

mestiza: a woman of mixed native and foreign ancestry.

mite: a very small creature.

mitt reader: palmist; palm reader.

pad room: room near the animals where pads, harness and tack for the elephants and horses are kept. It is not really a dressing room, though most of the animal people congregate there and might put their wardrobe there for the kickoff parade.

physiognomy: the features of somebody's face, especially when they are used as indicators of that person's character or temperament.

pony: a unit of measure for liquor; a glass or the amount of liquor it will hold, usually one ounce (29.6 ml).

proboscis: the elongated, protruding mouth parts of certain insects, adapted for sucking or piercing.

Prussian drill sergeant: a drill sergeant from Prussia. Prussia, a former northern European nation, based much of its rule on armed might, stressing rigid military discipline and maintaining one of the most strictly drilled armies in the world.

Punchinello: a comic character; Italian puppet character and probably the source of Punch, the chief male character of the Punch and Judy puppet show, dating back to the seventeenth century. He is the cruel and boastful husband of nagging wife Judy and the language is often coarse and satirical.

razorback: circus day laborer; man who loads and unloads railroad cars in a circus.

red light: a car; in the circus, this term is used when circus workers go to collect their pay and all they see are the red taillights of the employer's car receding in the distance as he drives away with all the payroll.

ringmaster: the circus Master of Ceremonies and main announcer. Originally, he stood in the center of the ring and paced the horses for the riding acts, keeping the horses running smoothly while performers did their tricks on the horses' backs.

rosinbacks: circus horses used for bareback riding, or the performers who ride them; the performing horses became known as "rosinbacks" by the circus personnel, after *rosin,* the non-slip foot powder placed on the horses' backs and used by the performers.

rubbering: rubbernecking; gawking or gaping; twisting or craning one's neck as if it were made of rubber in eager curiosity to see something.

rubber mules: work elephants.

sanctum sanctorum: an inviolably private place.

Scheherazade: the female narrator of *The Arabian Nights,* who during one thousand and one adventurous nights saved her life by entertaining her husband, the king, with stories.

shill: the cohort of a dishonest gambler; a circus employee who poses as a customer, plays a game (and is secretly allowed to win), or stands in line to make the box office look busy and motivate other customers to buy a ticket for the show.

slip artist: escape artist; a performer who entertains by escaping from confinement. Some of the performer's tricks are accomplished by illusionists' techniques.

spec: spectacle; the opening procession of a circus; a colorful pageant within the tent of all performers and animals in costume, usually at the beginning of the show. Used figuratively.

spots: circus music.

square-cube law: the way to calculate how much the surface area of an object changes as you scale its size up or down. This mathematical law states that the volume of an object (the size of the three-dimensional space occupied by the object) will change by the cube of the scale, while the surface area will change by the square of the scale; i.e., if a 2" square block is made twice as big (2 x 2), the surface area of the block will be four times as big, but the volume, and therefore the weight, will be eight times as much (2 x 2 x 2). If one kept increasing the block in this way, it would eventually collapse under its own weight. Conversely, if an object's size is halved, its structural strength (surface area) will be one-fourth of what it was, while its volume, and therefore its weight, will be only one-eighth of what it was. So, proportionally, it would be stronger.

SS: steamship.

stateroom: a private room or compartment on a train, ship, etc.

stern: the rear end of a ship or boat.

stint: a pause; halt.

stock: a kind of stiff, wide band or scarf for the neck.

strawberry shortcake: dishonest money.

swallow-tailed coat: a man's fitted coat, cut away over the hips and descending in a pair of tapering skirts behind. It is usually black and worn as part of full evening dress.

thistle chins: local residents.

van: vanguard; the forefront.

white wagon: the circus main office on the lot.

L. Ron Hubbard
in the Golden Age
of Pulp Fiction

In writing an adventure story
a writer has to know that he is adventuring
for a lot of people who cannot.
The writer has to take them here and there
about the globe and show them
excitement and love and realism.
As long as that writer is living the part of an
adventurer when he is hammering
the keys, he is succeeding with his story.

Adventuring is a state of mind.
If you adventure through life, you have a
good chance to be a success on paper.

Adventure doesn't mean globe-trotting,
exactly, and it doesn't mean great deeds.
Adventuring is like art.
You have to live it to make it real.

— L. RON HUBBARD

L. Ron Hubbard
and American
Pulp Fiction

B ORN March 13, 1911, L. Ron Hubbard lived a life at least as expansive as the stories with which he enthralled a hundred million readers through a fifty-year career.

Originally hailing from Tilden, Nebraska, he spent his formative years in a classically rugged Montana, replete with the cowpunchers, lawmen and desperadoes who would later people his Wild West adventures. And lest anyone imagine those adventures were drawn from vicarious experience, he was not only breaking broncs at a tender age, he was also among the few whites ever admitted into Blackfoot society as a bona fide blood brother. While if only to round out an otherwise rough and tumble youth, his mother was that rarity of her time—a thoroughly educated woman—who introduced her son to the classics of Occidental literature even before his seventh birthday.

But as any dedicated L. Ron Hubbard reader will attest, his world extended far beyond Montana. In point of fact, and as the son of a United States naval officer, by the age of eighteen he had traveled over a quarter of a million miles. Included therein were three Pacific crossings to a then still mysterious Asia, where he ran with the likes of Her British Majesty's agent-in-place

L. Ron Hubbard, left, at Congressional Airport, Washington, DC, 1931, with members of George Washington University flying club.

for North China, and the last in the line of Royal Magicians from the court of Kublai Khan. For the record, L. Ron Hubbard was also among the first Westerners to gain admittance to forbidden Tibetan monasteries below Manchuria, and his photographs of China's Great Wall long graced American geography texts.

Upon his return to the United States and a hasty completion of his interrupted high school education, the young Ron Hubbard entered George Washington University. There, as fans of his aerial adventures may have heard, he earned his wings as a pioneering barnstormer at the dawn of American aviation. He also earned a place in free-flight record books for the longest sustained flight above Chicago. Moreover, as a roving reporter for *Sportsman Pilot* (featuring his first professionally penned articles), he further helped inspire a generation of pilots who would take America to world airpower.

Immediately beyond his sophomore year, Ron embarked on the first of his famed ethnological expeditions, initially to then untrammeled Caribbean shores (descriptions of which would later fill a whole series of West Indies mystery-thrillers). That the Puerto Rican interior would also figure into the future of Ron Hubbard stories was likewise no accident. For in addition to cultural studies of the island, a 1932–33

LRH expedition is rightly remembered as conducting the first complete mineralogical survey of a Puerto Rico under United States jurisdiction.

There was many another adventure along this vein: As a lifetime member of the famed Explorers Club, L. Ron Hubbard charted North Pacific waters with the first shipboard radio direction finder, and so pioneered a long-range navigation system universally employed until the late twentieth century. While not to put too fine an edge on it, he also held a rare Master Mariner's license to pilot any vessel, of any tonnage in any ocean.

Yet lest we stray too far afield, there is an LRH note at this juncture in his saga, and it reads in part:

"I started out writing for the pulps, writing the best I knew, writing for every mag on the stands, slanting as well as I could."

To which one might add: His earliest submissions date from the summer of 1934, and included tales drawn from true-to-life Asian adventures, with characters roughly modeled on British/American intelligence operatives he had known in Shanghai. His early Westerns were similarly peppered with details drawn from personal experience. Although therein lay a first hard lesson from the often cruel world of the pulps. His first Westerns were soundly rejected as lacking the authenticity of a Max Brand yarn

Capt. L. Ron Hubbard in Ketchikan, Alaska, 1940, on his Alaskan Radio Experimental Expedition, the first of three voyages conducted under the Explorers Club flag.

(a particularly frustrating comment given L. Ron Hubbard's Westerns came straight from his Montana homeland, while Max Brand was a mediocre New York poet named Frederick Schiller Faust, who turned out implausible six-shooter tales from the terrace of an Italian villa).

Nevertheless, and needless to say, L. Ron Hubbard persevered and soon earned a reputation as among the most publishable names in pulp fiction, with a ninety percent placement rate of first-draft manuscripts. He was also among the most prolific, averaging between seventy and a hundred thousand words a month. Hence the rumors that L. Ron Hubbard had redesigned a typewriter for faster keyboard action and pounded out manuscripts on a continuous roll of butcher paper to save the precious seconds it took to insert a single sheet of paper into manual typewriters of the day.

That all L. Ron Hubbard stories did not run beneath said byline is yet another aspect of pulp fiction lore. That is, as publishers periodically rejected manuscripts from top-drawer authors if only to avoid paying top dollar, L. Ron Hubbard and company just as frequently replied with submissions under various pseudonyms. In Ron's case, the

A MAN OF MANY NAMES

Between 1934 and 1950, L. Ron Hubbard authored more than fifteen million words of fiction in more than two hundred classic publications. To supply his fans and editors with stories across an array of genres and pulp titles, he adopted fifteen pseudonyms in addition to his already renowned L. Ron Hubbard byline.

Winchester Remington Colt
Lt. Jonathan Daly
Capt. Charles Gordon
Capt. L. Ron Hubbard
Bernard Hubbel
Michael Keith
Rene Lafayette
Legionnaire 148
Legionnaire 14830
Ken Martin
Scott Morgan
Lt. Scott Morgan
Kurt von Rachen
Barry Randolph
Capt. Humbert Reynolds

list included: Rene Lafayette, Captain Charles Gordon, Lt. Scott Morgan and the notorious Kurt von Rachen—supposedly on the lam for a murder rap, while hammering out two-fisted prose in Argentina. The point: While L. Ron Hubbard as Ken Martin spun stories of Southeast Asian intrigue, LRH as Barry Randolph authored tales of

romance on the Western range—which, stretching between a dozen genres is how he came to stand among the two hundred elite authors providing close to a million tales through the glory days of American Pulp Fiction.

L. Ron Hubbard, circa 1930, at the outset of a literary career that would finally span half a century.

In evidence of exactly that, by 1936 L. Ron Hubbard was literally leading pulp fiction's elite as president of New York's American Fiction Guild. Members included a veritable pulp hall of fame: Lester "Doc Savage" Dent, Walter "The Shadow" Gibson, and the legendary Dashiell Hammett—to cite but a few.

Also in evidence of just where L. Ron Hubbard stood within his first two years on the American pulp circuit: By the spring of 1937, he was ensconced in Hollywood, adopting a Caribbean thriller for Columbia Pictures, remembered today as *The Secret of Treasure Island*. Comprising fifteen thirty-minute episodes, the L. Ron Hubbard screenplay led to the most profitable matinée serial in Hollywood history. In accord with Hollywood culture, he was thereafter continually called upon

111

The 1937 Secret of Treasure Island, *a fifteen-episode serial adapted for the screen by L. Ron Hubbard from his novel,* Murder at Pirate Castle.

to rewrite/doctor scripts—most famously for long-time friend and fellow adventurer Clark Gable.

In the interim—and herein lies another distinctive chapter of the L. Ron Hubbard story—he continually worked to open Pulp Kingdom gates to up-and-coming authors. Or, for that matter, anyone who wished to write. It was a fairly unconventional stance, as markets were already thin and competition razor sharp. But the fact remains, it was an L. Ron Hubbard hallmark that he vehemently lobbied on behalf of young authors—regularly supplying instructional articles to trade journals, guest-lecturing to short story classes at George Washington University and Harvard, and even founding his own creative writing competition. It was established in 1940, dubbed the Golden Pen, and guaranteed winners both New York representation and publication in *Argosy*.

But it was John W. Campbell Jr.'s *Astounding Science Fiction* that finally proved the most memorable LRH vehicle. While every fan of L. Ron Hubbard's galactic epics undoubtedly knows the story, it nonetheless bears repeating: By late 1938, the pulp publishing magnate of Street & Smith was determined to revamp *Astounding Science Fiction* for broader readership. In particular, senior editorial director F. Orlin Tremaine called for stories with a stronger *human element*. When acting editor John W. Campbell balked, preferring his spaceship-driven

112

tales, Tremaine enlisted Hubbard. Hubbard, in turn, replied with the genre's first truly *character-driven* works, wherein heroes are pitted not against bug-eyed monsters but the mystery and majesty of deep space itself—and thus was launched the Golden Age of Science Fiction.

The names alone are enough to quicken the pulse of any science fiction aficionado, including LRH friend and protégé, Robert Heinlein, Isaac Asimov, A. E. van Vogt and Ray Bradbury. Moreover, when coupled with LRH stories of fantasy, we further come to what's rightly been described as the foundation of every modern tale of horror: L. Ron Hubbard's immortal *Fear.* It was rightly proclaimed by Stephen King as one of the very few works to genuinely warrant that overworked term "classic"—as in: *"This is a classic tale of creeping, surreal menace and horror. . . . This is one of the really, really good ones."*

L. Ron Hubbard, 1948, among fellow science fiction luminaries at the World Science Fiction Convention in Toronto.

To accommodate the greater body of L. Ron Hubbard fantasies, Street & Smith inaugurated *Unknown*—a classic pulp if there ever was one, and wherein readers were soon thrilling to the likes of *Typewriter in the Sky* and *Slaves of Sleep* of which Frederik Pohl would declare: *"There are bits and pieces from Ron's work that became part of the language in ways that very few other writers managed."*

And, indeed, at J. W. Campbell Jr.'s insistence, Ron was regularly drawing on themes from the Arabian Nights and so introducing readers to a world of genies, jinn, Aladdin and Sinbad—all of which, of course, continue to float through cultural mythology to this day.

At least as influential in terms of post-apocalypse stories was L. Ron Hubbard's 1940 *Final Blackout*. Generally acclaimed as the finest anti-war novel of the decade and among the ten best works of the genre ever authored—here, too, was a tale that would live on in ways few other writers imagined.

Portland, Oregon, 1943; L. Ron Hubbard, captain of the US Navy subchaser PC 815.

Hence, the later Robert Heinlein verdict: "Final Blackout *is as perfect a piece of science fiction as has ever been written.*"

Like many another who both lived and wrote American pulp adventure, the war proved a tragic end to Ron's sojourn in the pulps. He served with distinction in four theaters and was highly decorated for commanding corvettes in the North Pacific. He was also grievously wounded in combat, lost many a close friend and colleague and thus resolved to say farewell to pulp fiction and devote himself to what it had supported these many years—namely, his serious research.

But in no way was the LRH literary saga at an end, for as he wrote some thirty years later, in 1980:

"Recently there came a period when I had little to do. This was novel in a life so crammed with busy years, and I decided to amuse myself by writing a novel that was pure *science fiction."*

114

That work was *Battlefield Earth: A Saga of the Year 3000*. It was an immediate *New York Times* bestseller and, in fact, the first international science fiction blockbuster in decades. It was not, however, L. Ron Hubbard's magnum opus, as that distinction is generally reserved for his next and final work: The 1.2 million word *Mission Earth*.

> **Final Blackout**
> *is as perfect a piece of science fiction as has ever been written.*
>
> —Robert Heinlein

How he managed those 1.2 million words in just over twelve months is yet another piece of the L. Ron Hubbard legend. But the fact remains, he did indeed author a ten-volume *dekalogy* that lives in publishing history for the fact that each and every volume of the series was also a *New York Times* bestseller.

Moreover, as subsequent generations discovered L. Ron Hubbard through republished works and novelizations of his screenplays, the mere fact of his name on a cover signaled an international bestseller. . . . Until, to date, sales of his works exceed hundreds of millions, and he otherwise remains among the most enduring and widely read authors in literary history. Although as a final word on the tales of L. Ron Hubbard, perhaps it's enough to simply reiterate what editors told readers in the glory days of American Pulp Fiction:

He writes the way he does, brothers, because he's been there, seen it and done it!

THE STORIES FROM THE GOLDEN AGE

Your ticket to adventure starts here with the Stories from
the Golden Age collection by master storyteller L. Ron Hubbard.
These gripping tales are set in a kaleidoscope of exotic locales and brim
with fascinating characters, including some of the
most vile villains, dangerous dames and brazen heroes
you'll ever get to meet.

The entire collection of over one hundred and fifty stories is being
released in a series of eighty books and audiobooks.
For an up to date listing of available titles,
go to www.goldenagestories.com.

AIR ADVENTURE

Arctic Wings	*Man-Killers of the Air*
The Battling Pilot	*On Blazing Wings*
Boomerang Bomber	*Red Death Over China*
The Crate Killer	*Sabotage in the Sky*
The Dive Bomber	*Sky Birds Dare!*
Forbidden Gold	*The Sky-Crasher*
Hurtling Wings	*Trouble on His Wings*
The Lieutenant Takes the Sky	*Wings Over Ethiopia*

FAR-FLUNG ADVENTURE

SEA ADVENTURE

TALES FROM THE ORIENT

MYSTERY

119

FANTASY

Borrowed Glory   *If I Were You*
The Crossroads   *The Last Drop*
Danger in the Dark   *The Room*
The Devil's Rescue   *The Tramp*
He Didn't Like Cats

SCIENCE FICTION

The Automagic Horse   *A Matter of Matter*
Battle of Wizards   *The Obsolete Weapon*
Battling Bolto   *One Was Stubborn*
The Beast   *The Planet Makers*
Beyond All Weapons   *The Professor Was a Thief*
A Can of Vacuum   *The Slaver*
The Conroy Diary   *Space Can*
The Dangerous Dimension   *Strain*
Final Enemy   *Tough Old Man*
The Great Secret   *240,000 Miles Straight Up*
Greed   *When Shadows Fall*
The Invaders

WESTERN

121